ONE WAY JOURNEY. . . .

Looking around him cautiously, Arthur left his
flat and walked the few yards to his Jag. Once
inside it he felt safe, but on the streets he knew he
was only too exposed. With a sigh of relief, he
inserted the key in the door, climbed in and sat
behind the wheel, his eyes closed and his
breathing deep.

'Hallo, Arthur.'

'Oh my Gawd!' For a moment Arthur felt as if he
was having the major coronary he had always
feared. He couldn't breathe and his whole body
was bathed in an instant cold sweat.

'Nice to see you out and about again.'

Arthur made an inarticulate noise that sounded
like the bleating of a wounded animal.

'Now we want you to drive us.'

Also by Anthony Masters in Sphere Books:

MINDER – BACK AGAIN

Minder

ANTHONY MASTERS

Based on the Minder series created by
Leon Griffiths and on the scripts written by
Leon Griffiths

SPHERE BOOKS LIMITED
London and Sydney

First published in Great Britain by
Sphere Books Ltd 1984
30–32 Gray's Inn Road, London WC1X 8JL
Copyright © Leon Griffiths Limited 1984
Reprinted 1984, 1985

TRADE
MARK

Set in 9/11 Century Schoolbook

Printed and bound in Great Britain by
Cox & Wyman Ltd, Reading

PART ONE

The occasion was not distinguished.

'It's a fight for the undiscerning fan,' said Arthur as he disconsolately watched the two fighters limping round the ring. It was a heavyweight bout and looked as if the two veterans were boxing from memory – from a distant memory. The punches were hard when they came but the gaps in between them seemed endless.

'Fair fight, eh?' commented Harry.

Arthur lit up a cigar and looked bleakly round at the grimy walls of the tatty hall. Then he turned back to watch the two boxers, one black, one white, as they clumsily slugged it out.

'They're not exactly class, are they?'

Harry grinned and pulled up the collar of his grubby raincoat. It was cold in the hall and he felt chilled to the bone.

'That's not the point, Arthur,' said Harry. 'Those guys are giving good value, aren't they? They like fighting – they don't like each other. That's how all Eric's bills score.'

'Yeah,' said Arthur. 'I'm sure you're right.'

'Here comes the action,' said Harry, sucking in his breath. 'I like it.'

The black fighter had just landed a haymaker on the white fighter who was even now reeling across the ring on legs like jelly. He landed on the bottom rope and stayed there, swaying. He didn't fall down but neither did he have the energy to get up. The black fighter closed in for the kill and it was all over.

Arthur winced as the final blows rained in.

'Do you reckon he'll get up?' Harry asked with mild curiosity.

'He shouldn't have come in the first place,' said Arthur, relighting a sodden cigar.

Harry watched the final body-blow, and then said:

'How's Terry?'

'In the pink.'

'Terry would have loved this.'

'Would he?'

'Yeah – great fighter was Tel. You know –'

'What?'

'Eric would give him a chance.'

3

'What at?'

'The fight game, Arthur. You're not concentrating, are you?'

'What on earth would Terry want here?'

'Eric would give him a bash. He'll take on anybody – bouncers, minders, old fighters, has-beens –'

'Has-beens?' asked Arthur quickly. There was an edge to his voice.

'Oh – I don't mean that about Terry. What I'm trying to tell you is that Eric likes a guy with heart. Heart and bottle.'

Arthur laughed angrily. 'Do you really think Terry would degrade himself by joining a blood and snot circus like this?'

'Just asking, Arthur. That's all – just asking.'

'Well, don't ask.'

'But he still does a bit, doesn't he?'

'Well – he takes care of people from time to time. Then again he might supervise some premises. But most of the time he improves himself.'

'What at, Arthur?'

'Evening classes, or something.'

'Blimey.'

'You see, Harry, you got my Terence all wrong. Haven't you?'

'If you say so, Arthur.'

The white fighter was now lying on the floor of the boxing ring, whilst the scattered crowd gave vent to tepid applause. The black fighter, meanwhile, had retired to his corner and was going through a ritual of clumsy jubilation.

'My boy's not for this,' insisted Arthur. 'He's in a different league.'

Harry kept quiet. He knew when Arthur was making up his mind.

'Get out and shut up!'

Terry dragged the two young hooligans towards the door of the pub.

'All I did was to play the juke box,' protested one of them.

'With your Doc Martins? You're out.'

'I left a pint of lager on the bar.'

4

'You threw it at the barman. Remember? That's why you're leaving.'

'Yeah?'

They were at the open doorway now and Terry suddenly released his hold.

'It's bye-bye time.'

'We'll get you.'

'Naughty.'

But at that moment one of the yobboes twisted round in a highly acrobatic manner, aiming a back kick at Terry as he did so.

'Blimey,' said Terry, as he caught the blow on his elbow. He hadn't been expecting that – not from a kid. At once they ran off and for a moment Terry wondered if he should go after them. Then he decided against it. His elbow hurt too much, and, besides, he was knackered. Those lousy yobs were getting him down and there was no doubt that a combination of small-time bouncing and minding for Arthur was driving him spare. There must be more to life than this, he mused, rubbing his elbow as he walked back into the garish din of the pub.

'Had a bit of trouble?' asked the barman.

'Nothing I couldn't sort out.'

'Oh yes – looks as if someone's upset you.'

'It's the job that gets me down,' said Terry.

'This job – or the other one?'

'All the jobs get me down.'

'Why not go to the Job Centre, then?'

'Eh?'

'The Job Centre – you know – where you get jobs.'

'I just might give it a try.'

Arthur and Harry sat and waited for the next attraction as the dazed and bloodied white boxer was led past them by his seconds.

'I thought you'd like the bill,' said Harry hopefully, but Arthur was not to be drawn into an optimistic conversation.

'I don't know why they didn't have the fight in the gutter – it's where it belonged.'

5

'Or in the road,' returned Harry. 'Like in the old days.'

Arthur relit his cigar gloomily. 'What old days?'

'The 'thirties – when blokes fought it out on the street corner for a few pennies.'

'Very nice.'

"Think of the nostalgia –'

'I am.'

'Now, why don't you have a chat with Eric? You're a man who likes to make the odd pound – and Eric likes spending it. You two should get on like a pair of love-birds. You'll soon be billing and cooing at each other like nobody's business.'

'Will we?'

'By the way,' said Harry, changing the subject hastily, 'you still into property?'

'I dabble, Harry. I sometimes dabble.'

'Well – I got a very nice modernised flat – clean as a whistle with a lovely postal code.'

'Why do you want to sell?' asked Arthur with just a hint of suspicion in his voice.

Harry cleared his throat.

'My Marge has pushed off with a double-glazing sales-man.'

'No!'

'She was as loyal as a spaniel.'

'That's a charming picture.'

'Thank God I've got the lease in my name, but I couldn't live there.'

'Why ever not? Thought you liked it there?'

'Be sensitive, Arthur – there's too many memories – and the new double glazing! I'm going back to me little bed-sit.'

For the first time that evening, Arthur began to look interested.

'How much money are we talking about?'

'Search me, Arthur. I'm out of touch. Of course – it's not been an easy life, particularly with that little stretch in Hull. Everyone knew I was innocent.'

'Yes,' said Arthur, 'any decent liberal Judge would have ignored all that evidence about the shotgun in the car boot.'

'I even had a brace of grouse in there and all.'

6

'Pity they were out of season, Harry. Now – this flat –'

But Harry was already looking at the next two boxers who were climbing into the ring. Flabby and overweight, they looked finished before they had started.

'Give 'em a bus pass each – and some supplementary benefits. That's what they really need,' remarked Arthur, still thinking about the flat.

'Don't knock it, Arthur. There's plenty of loot in this game.'

The two boxers lumbered clumsily towards each other.

Has he bitten? Harry wondered. If so – it could be a bite at two cherries.

Arthur Daley sat in the back of a taxi, wondering about Harry's flat. There could be something in it – something worth following up. He was feeling the pinch at the moment and needed something to happen. In fact, life had been so slow that it had hardly been worthwhile Terry minding him over the last few weeks. Gazing vacantly from the taxi window, Arthur's mind ran over a dozen potential money-making schemes, but they were all schemes he had tried before – schemes that had failed and were not likely to respond to the kiss of life. Gloomily he continued to stare out into the street – until he saw Terry. For a moment, Arthur could hardly believe his own eyes. Terry was standing outside a Job Centre, studying the notices in the window. Then, to Arthur's horror, he went inside.

'Oi!' yelled Arthur, but to no avail. The street was empty. Then he turned to the cabbie and excitedly asked him to stop. Grudgingly, the cabbie pulled up and Arthur tumbled out in a highly ruffled state.

'I'll be back in a minute.'

'Hold on.'

'Eh?'

'Now look – our destination was Berkeley Square and now you're going into a Job Centre.'

'I'll be back in a minute, I tell you.'

'I'll have the fare now.'

Arthur turned on him indignantly, panting slightly with his hat askew, as he stood agitatedly by the side of the cab.

'You think I'm going to do a runner?'

'*I* don't know, do I?'

'A man of my calibre. I'm an employ*er* – not an employ*ee*.'

'I don't care if you're the Chairman of the Board – I want the fare.'

Arthur dug reluctantly into his pocket and produced some loose coins.

'You don't expect a tip for this, do you?'

The cabbie pocketed the money and grinned.

'I don't expect you'll get a job, either.'

Arthur came quietly up behind Terry, who was examining the cards inside the Job Centre with grave interest.

'I can't believe I'd ever see you in such a humiliating position – I really can't, Terry. So, it's dossing under the arches next, is it?'

Terry went on looking at the cards, without the slightest reaction to Arthur's tirade.

'The idea of you – you of all people – being *here*. My friend, my associate – the boy I brought in from the gutter, nursed, trained and taught.'

Still Terry said nothing.

'I mean – look at that lot. Maggie's millions.'

Terry turned on Arthur with a patient smile. 'Look, Arthur – all I'm doing is sussing out the job market.'

Arthur gave him an outraged look, as if he was committing a sacrilege. Then he turned to the notice-board with contempt.

'Look at 'em – motor cycle messengers and audio-typists. My God, Terry, is this the end of your ambitions? These aren't for you – these are for *workers, civilians*, the *hoi polloi*. This is *work*.' Arthur made the word '*work*' sound like an obscenity.

But Arthur did not succeed with his attempt to inspire Terry. He merely succeeded in annoying him.

'Look, Arthur – just button it, will you?' said Terry. 'I've had enough of being on the door in the Acton khazi, facing up to lippy hooligans and getting Kung Fu kicks on the shoulder. I've just got myself a season ticket to the casualty unit – and it's not something I wanted. I'm also broke.'

Arthur smiled bravely, anxious to placate Terry and knowing how to do it.

'Now, why didn't you say, Tel. Look at this,' he bent over one of the cards, lighting his cigar and dropping ash on it, 'look at this – handyman for a block of flats. That's not so bad, is it?'

Terry ignored his sarcasm and moved over to another card. It read:

> PLAYLEADER
> ARE YOU GOOD WITH CHILDREN?
> A NEW ADVENTURE PLAYGROUND
> NEEDS A PLAYLEADER. RELIABLE,
> RESPONSIBLE, PATIENT. WOULD
> SUIT AN ACTIVE YOUNG MAN AND/
> OR PHYSICAL EDUCATION INSTRUCTOR.
> ASK FOR DETAILS AT DESK.

Without comment, Terry walked straight over to the desk, where an attractive young woman had just finished dealing with another client. Arthur watched him go uneasily. Just as he was about to follow him, he felt a hand on his shoulder and turned quickly.

'Hallo, Arthur. Long time no see.' The middle-aged man seemed highly amused to see Arthur in such unlikely surroundings. 'Now, what chance have the likes of us got if you're down here after a job as an audio-typist?'

Arthur frowned, unwilling to see any humour in the situation. He felt insecure in this place, where offers of work – the wrong kind of work – surrounded him. 'Do I look like a man after a job? I've got two employment agencies of me own – what would I want a job for?'

'Well, Arthur –'

'Now, if you register at my office and give me a pony – you could be a Marketing Director in Milton Keynes.'

'You must be joking.'

Arthur pulled out a business card and gave it to him grandly. 'It's only up-market jobs with me. Not like all this rubbish here.'

Reading from the card, the man slowly intoned:
'The Boardroom Sauna Club.'

Arthur looked slightly confused. 'Eh? Oh. I see. You'd better keep that one – never know when it might come in useful.' He quickly produced another card, gave it to the man and then walked towards the counter, where Terry was engaged in earnest conversation with the girl. Terry was explaining that he didn't have any qualifications, but he had been a boxer – and had helped to teach self-defence in a youth club.

Arthur listened in silence for a while, but suddenly could bear it no longer. 'Never mind that,' he said brusquely 'he's got a job.'

'Ignore him,' said Terry.

'And as for youth activities – ask him why he beat up a couple of juveniles last night.'

'I'll chin you,' put in Terry menacingly.

But Arthur ploughed on: 'See how aggressive he is, miss. Now, this boy's had a very deprived childhood and no way could he be a playleader. Besides – as I say – he's got a job.'

Terry turned to Arthur reluctantly. 'What job?' he said blankly.

But Arthur was determined to sustain the moment of interest. Arthur still addressed the girl. 'You see, miss – he gets two grand for fifteen minutes.'

Terry smiled understandingly and turned back to the girl. 'The man's a nutter,' he said.

'So, forget about audio-typing and climbing up ropes. Put it this way – this man thought the Job Centre was a new boutique. Look at his schmutter – not my style, but he likes it. All Pierre Amies and Yves Lawrence Corner.'

The girl looked fascinated but Terry raised his eyebrows and Arthur continued.

'You see, lovey, I'm his guvnor and I pay his stamps.'

'Why do you do that?' asked Terry.

'You see,' Arthur continued to address himself to the girl, 'he's not one of three million unemployed – he's a fraud. Don't be misled by the way he looks.'

'Shut up, Arthur.'

'And now, Terence, I bring you tidings of great joy.' Arthur gave Terry a beatific and beguiling smile. He paused and there was a long, awkward silence. Finally Terry broke it:

'I'll have to have a word with him,' he said reluctantly to the girl.

'I would,' she said enthusiastically, 'it sounds – intriguing.'

'You don't know him like I do.'

'Why don't you come back and tell me what happens?'

Terry paused whilst Arthur's smile froze.

'Don't mind if I do. How about six o'clock?'

'Fine.'

'I'll even buy you a drink.'

'I'd like that.'

Arthur put his arm protectively round Terry's shoulders. He turned to the girl like a king. 'You see – I come in and you get a result.' He gently turned Terry away from the counter and began to lead him towards the door.

'Why does an intelligent kid like her work in a place like this?'

Ten minutes later, Arthur and Terry were sitting in the back of a cab in the heart of dockland. Arthur gave the impression of being full of largesse, but it was at times like this that Terry was at his most wary.

'Well?'

Arthur lit a new cigar, taking his time about it. Then he said: 'You're fit, aren't you?'

'I'm fit.'

'Course, some fighters are a bit like good claret. They mature. Now, just cast your mind back to good old Archie Moore. Almost fifty – and he was still slugging.'

'Pity he didn't knock anyone down.'

'Then there was Jersey Joe Walcott. What a punch.'

'He was punch-drunk.'

'I went along to one of those pirate shows last night. You know, unlicensed.'

'That figures.'

'The wife could have knocked out most of 'em.'

'Arthur – no!' Realism dawned and it made Terry want to throw up.

'They were bums, Tel. Walk-ons.'

'And I'm one of them?'

'No – you had class. You wouldn't even sweat – and you know I love you like a son.'

'Let your son do it.'

'They're giving money away. Now – don't you owe me a favour?'

'I done a favour seven years ago. Remember?'

'For some very influential people, Tel.'

'They were great. This ain't your night, they said. I had to hold the guy up for seven rounds.'

'The price was good.'

'You should 'ave taken care of me.'

'I didn't know you then.'

'But I could have been somebody then. I could have been a contender.'

'You're not with me. You *were* the contender – that was the whole point, son.'

'Oh, yeah.'

'You were to lose to whats-is-name Wilson. Then he'd be a contender with a quick return bout. You could have murdered him. But what did you do instead? Went in like a dying swan!'

'I got resin in me eye.'

'Yeah? You was like Sir John Gielgud on a bad night. They should have nicked you for over-acting instead of just taking your licence away.'

'So, what happened?' said Terry bitterly, 'Wilson becomes a champ.'

'An ageing rabbit.' Arthur paused reflectively. 'You got your money, didn't you?'

'Did I, hell? They took the purse away. Your mate said the bookies wouldn't pay out.'

Arthur winced. 'I forgot that, Tel. But now I remember I lost more than you. Much more. No wonder you owe me a favour.'

'Blimey – you do come it, don't you?'

'Look – the motor's in dock and I've got problems.'

'Problems?'

'Like forty videos of *E.T.* with no ending.'

'Yeah?'

'And what about forty gross of denim shirts?'

'What's wrong with 'em?'

'What's right? They've got nine-inch collars and thirty-six inch sleeves. Do for a midget with extra-long arms.'

'That's your problem, Arthur.'

'I should be taking that playleader job. Not you.'

'I'd love to see you on a rope.'

Arthur paused reflectively. 'Alf was champion of the world when he was older than you, Terry.'

'Great.'

'And there's always Sylvia.'

'Sylvia?'

'Sylvia what's-it. Rocky. I mean – I know it was only a film. But where are your dreams, Tel? In audio-typing? In swinging on ropes? You should have a dog, like Rocky's'.

'Look, Arthur. I've got plenty of friends. I don't need you to look after me. Not like this anyway. Me friends can.'

'Oh, Terry. But tell me one thing?'

'What?'

'Where are your friends now?' Arthur rapped on the cab's partition. 'I'll pick up my own motor now,' he said grandly.

When Arthur had collected the souped up Jaguar that he drove so erratically through the London traffic, he headed for Harry's flat. Once in there, he was almost asphyxiated by the unwashed smell of the place. Dirty shirts and socks littered the main room and the furniture was both tatty and broken. Harry was in a vest and old grey trousers with greasy looking slippers on his bare feet.

'You look a real picture,' said Arthur.

'I was going to tidy up –'

'So this is why they call you Dirty Harry.' Arthur looked round and sniffed, wrinkling up his nose in distaste.

'I used to be a ringer for Clint Eastwood,' volunteered Harry. 'Mind you – he's a bit taller, isn't he?'

Arthur smiled. 'The man wouldn't hang his poncho in this gaff – any chance of opening a window?'

Harry moved obligingly to the window and began to struggle with the frame. But it would not budge and he retreated hopelessly.

'I don't like draughts,' he said.

'It's a nice flat,' said Arthur looking gloomily at the window. 'Tight?'

'Since she left, I've let the place go. I don't even do much hoovering.'

'I had noticed. Ever thought of a dustpan?'

'She took it with her.'

'Now, Harry,' Arthur laid a fatherly hand on Harry's grubby shoulder, then quickly took it away – 'you can buy dustpans nowadays.' Arthur looked around him again, with a grimace. 'So this is the flat that's on the market?'

'Lease and fittings.'

'Fittings?'

Harry looked unhappy. 'Furniture too.'

'So you call this furniture? How would you describe it? Middle-period Hilda Ogden?'

'It's all good stuff.'

'It's not worth a penny.'

'Arthur –'

'It's drek, Harry. All drek!'

'It's a nice address.' Harry waved to a newspaper laden sofa. 'Why don't you sit down?' He began to push the newspapers on to the floor. Beneath them was an old pair of underpants. Arthur remained standing.

'I haven't seen the cat for a week,' muttered Harry.

'Probably suffocated somewhere,' suggested Arthur. 'Or gone down the Welfare.'

'What about the Arabs then?' asked Harry, clearing away some dirty plates and a lethal-looking can of half-opened sardines. 'They're always looking for flats.'

'They wouldn't stable their camels in here.' Arthur sighed and sat down on the sofa. He quickly rose again as there was a snapping sound from the springs. 'What about the rent? Is it controlled?'

'Oh, yes,' said Harry, a little too quickly.

'And the lease?'

'My solicitor's drawing it up.'

'How much?'

'Ten grand.'

'Three – it's all it's worth.'

'It's only ten minutes from the West End.'

'It's a doss-house. Three and a half.'

'I was thinking of six.'

'When even the cat's left?'

'I can't accept that, Arthur.'

'Look – I'll give you three thousand seven hundred and fifty. How about that, Harry?'

'That's unacceptable, Arthur.'

'I'll never be a rich man with this kind of generosity.'

'It's not enough, Arthur.'

'But it's a deal, isn't it, Harry?'

That night Terry took the girl from the Job Centre down to the Winchester Club for a drink. Her name was Nicky and Terry hoped he was on to a winner.

'Do you want a table – or shall we sit at the bar?' he asked her, hoping that he would not have to introduce her to the all-knowing barman, Dave. Luckily she suggested a table and Terry was able to face Dave alone.

'You've just missed Arthur.'

'Good. Gin and tonic for the lady – and I'll have a pint of lager.'

'You won't.'

'Eh?'

'The lady can have what she likes. But you're on orange juice.'

'What the hell for?'

'Arthur says.'

A blind fury seized Terry and he immediately wanted to do something violent – preferably to Arthur.

'You've gotta lose at least twelve pounds,' said Dave.

'What's all this about?'

'Your comeback. Arthur reckons you're about ready.'

'I'll kill him.'

'It's the other guy you've gotta kill.'

'He's got no damn right to –'

'Arthur's very keen.'

'Arthur – bloody Arthur is on the make. Again.'

'How can you misunderstand him so?' Dave grinned and started polishing glasses. Something in his confident movements made Terry feel he was arguing a lost cause.

'I am *not* boxing,' said Terry very slowly and clearly. 'I've retired.'

'That's what I said to Arthur.'

'Licensed *or* unlicensed.'

'You know what Arthur said?'

'I don't *want* to know what Arthur said.'

'He said: "We'll win." That's what he said.'

'We?'

'He's afraid you'll lose your bottle. Now – what was it? ' Vera and Harmonic for the lady – and an orange juice for you.'

Terry glanced at Dave. Then a strange feeling of familiarity flooded over him.

'I've been here before,' he muttered to himself.

Arthur's alarm went off at ten to six and he woke blearily, knowing there was something important to do. He slept alone, his wife having elected years ago to move into the next bedroom. This suited Arthur for various reasons, an important one being that he was free to use the phone at any time of the night without interference.

Gradually, Arthur began to wake, remembering with an exhilaration that he had not felt for months, that he had a new job for Terry. He dialled his number.

'Yeah?' Terry's voice was sleepy and churlish.

'You alone?'

There was silence. Then Terry said ungraciously: 'What the hell do you want?'

'It's six o'clock and the air is clean. No traffic, no carbon monoxide –'

'You gone crazy?'

'No – I'm very comfortable here, snuggled up in my pit.'

'Why not get some more kip? I could do with some.'

'But you should be up.'

'What?'

'In a track suit with a woolly hat.'

'You *are* crazy.'

'And heavy boots.'

'Arthur –'

'You should be pounding the streets, my son.'

'I'm not going back into it.'

'Five miles good run and then a nice cuppa tea.'

'Get off the phone, Arthur.'

'Quick half-hour of breakfast TV and into the gym.'

'Push off!'

'Punish yourself, Terence. And get up this second!'

With a smile Arthur replaced the receiver on a string of expletives from an enraged Terry.

Terry buried his face in the pillow and pulled the eiderdown over his head. He was determined to resist Arthur's pressure. He remembered the humiliation of his last time in the ring – and thought again of the unhappy way that all Arthur's plans had of backfiring with himself as victim. This time he was determined that Arthur would not succeed in persuading him into disaster.

Arthur and Harry were standing opposite a shabby door between two shops. On the door was a small, grubby notice. It read:

NATIONAL ASSOCIATION OF FAIR FIGHTING

'There you are,' said Harry in a proprietorial manner.

'Very nice too,' replied Arthur.

'That's Eric all over.'

'What's Eric all over?'

'Fair,' said Harry. 'You won't regret getting into this, Arthur.'

Arthur clapped his hand on Harry's shoulder, ' *You* might, Harry boy. *You* might.'

Eric Morgan's appearance cheered Arthur up when they met him in his tiny, cluttered office at the top of a long flight of narrow stairs. He was in his early thirties and had a pink, freshly scrubbed look that went well with his lilting Welsh accent and stockbroker style. A slightly ageing whiz-kid, he certainly knew how to chat up Arthur. Shaking hands with him vigorously, Eric said, 'Arthur Daley – a legend in your own life-time. Do you know – my Da even used to talk about you?'

'Did he now?' Arthur smiled horribly. 'I knew quite a few Taffs in those days.' He winced as the handshake continued and was then mercifully terminated.

'Still,' said Eric with his too easy smile, 'count your fingers, though,' he said.

'I'm an open book. How is your old fella?'

'Still in Broadmoor.' Eric turned grandiosely to Harry. 'Be a good boy and go and get a cup of tea somewhere.'

'If you insist,' replied Harry and made a slow and reluctant exit.

When he had gone, Eric said to Arthur: 'I want to be a millionaire before I'm thirty-five.'

'We all wanted to be that when we were young,' said Arthur in a fatherly tone.

'Didn't you miss out?' replied Eric sweetly.

Arthur suddenly itched to wipe the smile off Eric's face, but he was not a man of violence. He considered that to be Terry's province. 'I get by. Quite well.'

Eric smiled. Arthur knew he was going to find this rather superior aloof smile very irritating in future.

'You see, Arthur,' said Eric, 'I'm a radical. I'm for alternative boxing and I'm against the establishment.'

'You one of the militant tendency then?'

'Power to the people.'

'That's what I say.'

'My Da had some strange ideas.'

'He would have – being in Broadmoor and all that. No disrespect, mind you.'

'My Da thought of boxing as folk art.'

'Oh yeah?'

'All those after-dinner shows they have now. It's elitist crap. What I want – what the people want – is legalised street corner scraps! Are we speaking the same language, Arthur?'

'Well – I like a bit of skill, you know.'

'Skill?' Eric looked outraged. 'Skill's for snooker. I want blood. Blood, Arthur.' He thumped on the desk to underline his words.

Arthur nodded uneasily. 'I like a bit of claret myself. Talking of drinking –'

'Don't touch it. Tell you what – I'll give you a grand for your boy.'

Arthur laughed lightly as if Eric had made a tiny joke. 'Terry wouldn't demean himself.'

'Not for a grand?'

'Not a chance.'

'You know Jackie Wilson –' Eric's voice was a little on edge and Arthur felt a warm glow creeping over him.

'Wilson? Terry would have to prop him up for seven rounds.'

'But would it be an attraction?'

Arthur considered, 'I'd sell a couple of hundred tickets myself.'

'Then, you've got two grand!'

'And a half?'

'The fight's not at the Albert Hall.'

'What do you want?' asked Arthur slowly. 'Blood or "Beethoven's Fifth"?'

Eric stared hard at him and Arthur knew the vital moment had come.

'OK,' said Eric reluctantly, 'you've got yourself a deal.'

With a squeal of tyres Arthur pulled up the Jag outside Terry's flat, and climbed out. For a moment he stood, wide-eyed with sheer astonishment, at the extraordinary sight that greeted him.

'What the hell are you doing?'

'Grafting,' said Terry. He was sitting on the first floor sill, cleaning the windows.

'You'll do yourself a mischief.'

19

'I never knew you cared.'

'Oh, but I do care, Tel. I do care very much.' Arthur came and stood below him, looking up in great, slightly flushed, concern. 'Get down,' he said, 'now.'

'Why?'

'As your manager – I insist you get down!'

'As my what?'

'You heard.' Arthur lit a cigar. 'We got money in the bank – and Jackie Wilson to fight.'

'Who?'

'Yeah – that'll make you drop your chammy.'

'Arthur –'

'Now be friendly, Tel. Don't tell me to go away.'

'Go away, Arthur.'

Terry swung himself back over the sill and into his flat. Arthur hurried inside and up the stairs. Puffing slightly, he let himself in. Terry was sitting on the bed, looking suspicious. 'What are you on about, Arthur?'

'Wait till I get my breath.'

'You're not fit, Arthur.'

'Window cleaning?' Arthur sat heavily down in a chair. 'Yesterday it was audio-typing and swinging on ropes. Today it's window cleaning.'

'They're my windows.'

'So it's a pirate show.' Arthur stretched out his legs and puffed out cigar smoke in a luxuriant cloud. 'But you're top of the bill.'

'No.'

'Had a better offer?'

'No.'

'What have you got? One night stand on the door of the disco?'

Terry said nothing.

'Diary full?'

Terry said nothing.

'I'm offering you dignity –'

Still Terry said nothing.

'Respect.'

'Are you kidding?'

'Money.'

Terry was silent again but Arthur could see that he was thinking.

'You don't have any money right now. Do you, Terry?'

Terry was still thinking.

'You've got your old dressing gown, haven't you? With your name on the back? I'll even take it to the cleaners. Personally, Hey –' The light of inspiration came into Arthur's eyes. 'How about sponsorship? Nick the cleaner would love that. I can see the wording now – Two hour service . . . Alterations our speciality . . . Try our new luxury shirt service . . .'

'There's no space across the shoulders,' said Terry.

'Then let's shove it on your backside! Blimey, Tel – you could be a walking industry.'

Glumly, Terry moved to the kitchen area, where two used tea-bags sat equally glumly on the draining board.

'Do you want some second-hand tea?'

'You're top of the bill, Tel.' Arthur rose to his feet, pushing home his advantage.

'You're with Jackie Wilson.'

Silence.

'He's ex-champion of Britain. Ex-champion of the Commonwealth.' Arthur paused dramatically.

'Why's he doing it?' asked Terry, for the first time showing a flicker of interest.

'Because like many good men before him he frittered his wealth away.'

'Oh yeah.'

'Boozing all night. Badly advised business ventures. Fair-weather friends who didn't have an umbrella between them.'

'I've heard it all before,' said Terry, putting on the kettle.

'Of course you have, Tel,' replied Arthur, laying a fatherly hand on his arm. 'It's the old, old story. In the immortal words of Willie Pep – "First you lose your legs and then you lose your friends." ' Arthur paused for that to sink in. Then he spoke quickly and decisively. 'You've got a month.'

Terry was silent again. Then he said:

'This guy, Wilson —'

'Yes Tel?'

'He owes me, doesn't he?'

'Course he does. You made him.'

'I mean — I could've been a champ.'

'Course you could, boy. But you can have your chance again.'

'I don't —'

'Be positive, Tel. *Think* positive.'

'I can't help remembering what happened the first time around.'

'Forget it. I'm gonna look after you. And besides —'

'Besides what?'

'Think of the money.'

'How much, Arthur?'

'Enough to buy you some new tea-bags, Tel.'

Gradually, if reluctantly, Terry began to accept Arthur's idea. It was at least a better idea than earning lousy money doing lousy jobs and getting kicked in the elbow for his trouble.

'You've got a month.' Arthur's voice echoed in Terry's mind as he prepared for his first training work-out. It was early — horribly, unaccustomedly early as Terry pounded the dew-fresh streets of Fulham. He wore a track suit, a towel round his neck and a pair of the heaviest boots he could find. The streets were empty and although he began to sweat very quickly, Terry felt a sense of exhilaration as he thundered over the pavements. He was breathing hard and the exhilaration was beginning to leave him as the car slowly passed him. This was getting too much like hard work, thought Terry, and the memory of other similar mornings filtered gloomily into his mind.

Twenty-five yards ahead, Terry noticed that the car had stopped. As he drew abreast of it, a familiar face gazed up at him.

'I trust we are not fleeing from the scene of the crime.'

'With these boots?' Terry came to a relieved halt.

Detective Constable Rycott smiled sadly. 'Why not? If I see someone in unusual garb at six o'clock in the morning in a residential area – it is my duty to take note.'

'I'm training.'

'Quite. But what for?'

'I'm making me come back.'

'Oh yeah.'

'I've got a fight in a month.' As he said the words Terry felt a sense of pride.

'Didn't you have a fight last week?'

'This is different. It's boxing – the fight game.'

'Where is your venue, young man?'

'I dunno. Ilford maybe.'

'A couple of "briefs" for your local custodians of law and order might be a nice idea.'

'That's Arthur's department.'

'In that case it'll cost me the Royal box!'

Terry grinned. 'It's going to cost a bleeding orange box for you, Mr Rycott.'

'Isn't that nice? Do you know – if I wasn't on me way home – I could nick you.'

'What for?'

'Anything really. Loitering with intent. Parking on a double yellow line. It hasn't been much of a week for me.'

'No?'

'It's been slow. What I could have done with was a nice bank robbery and a couple of transvestites kidnapping the Mayor.'

'So sorry.'

'I haven't been in the local paper for months.'

'I'll put the whisper round for you.'

'I'd be grateful. Now, on your way, Terry. I'd like to see you work up a good sweat.'

With a groan Terry pounded into action again and for a few minutes, Detective Constable Rycott kerb-crawled beside him.

'Go it, Tel!'

'You're a right sod, you are.'

'Now, now – insulting language to a police officer.'

23

After a while Rycott drove away, leaving Terry to his solitary sweating.

Three quarters of an hour later, Terry arrived back at his flat. He felt terrible, light-headed with exhaustion. In fact he was so shattered that he did not see Arthur's Jag parked in the entrance.

'Gawd help us,' said a familiar voice.

Terry lay back in his chair, too exhausted to even unlace his boots.

'Make some tea,' he gasped.

'I've had tea,' said Arthur cheerfully. 'Couple of rashers, scrambled eggs – and a slice of toast.'

'Tea,' moaned Terry.

'What a two and eight. Do you know – I've got more of a chance of beating Jackie Wilson than you. Look at the state you're in.'

'I'm out of practice.' Giving up Arthur's potential tea-making abilities as a lost cause, Terry stumbled to the kettle.

'I'll have coffee,' said Arthur.

Terry said something unintelligible.

'What was that, son?'

'Nothing, Arthur.' Silence.

'What you need is a trainer.'

'I'm training meself. I do know a bit more about boxing than you do, Arthur.'

'You reckon?'

'Yes, Arthur.'

'I know more about everything than you do, Terry. History, current affairs, motors, politics, hang-gliding, the fine arts – but particularly about the noble art. Now you tell me – who was the only man who won the World Heavyweight title when he was on the canvas?'

Terry said nothing.

'Got yer, haven't I? Max Schmeling won the title from Jack Sharkey on a foul. You didn't know that, did you? Now give me another one.'

Terry handed Arthur a cup of instant coffee.

'I'll find you a trainer.'

'I said I can train meself, Arthur.'

'Look, son – as your manager *I* call the shots. So I chose Soldier Atkins.'

Terry laughed mockingly. 'Not old Soldier?'

'He's the best.'

'Three score and ten and plus.'

'Don't you knock the old-uns. They know what's what.'

'So here we are down memory lane,' began Terry.

But Arthur frowned over his coffee.

'Terence – you want to win this fight?'

'Yes. That's why I don't want Soldier Atkins.'

'If you want to win you have to trust your manager, and Soldier Atkins it's gonna be.'

Terence began to mimic Soldier: 'Old Tommy Farr said to me . . . and Len Harvey, what a gentleman . . .'

'Old Tommy Farr, now he could have a fight. Nobody could take liberties with Tommy. And then Len Harvey – what a gentleman – in and out of the ring – and with the sweetest straight left in the world.'

Terry glanced ironically at Arthur as Soldier went into his familiar anecdotes but Arthur stolidly ignored him. Around them the gym was full of action, with the heavy bags being thumped and with the staccato fire of the speed-ball pummelling their ear-drums.

Arthur turned to Terry and beamed at him.

'See he knows it all. Don't you Soldier?'

Soldier, an upright, elderly man with a military air replied: 'It's in me bones, Arthur.'

'And the family – eh Soldier?' Arthur sounded like the benevolent superintendent of an old people's home.

Soldier beamed happily. 'My dear old Mum weighed in at eleven stone seven pounds – your kind of stamp, Terry, and a very similar style – a real walk-in fighter was the old lady. She was the undisputed champion of the Co-op queue during the war.'

Terry looked at Arthur, and then at Soldier. He seemed

restless. 'No disrespect, Soldier. But what exactly are you gonna do for me?'

'I'm going to make you a winner, son.'

'But –'

'People say the last fight was hooky.'

'You can say that again.'

'You were on a hiding to nothing,' said Soldier in a derisive tone.

'It was a set-up,' replied Terry.

'A bit of villainy.' Soldier cleared his throat. 'Maybe they wanted to be sure.'

'I had him all over the place.'

'You simple-minded?' said Soldier with sudden contempt.

Terry turned to Arthur, 'You tell him.'

But Arthur merely looked uncomfortable 'Well – he was the favourite. Er – Wilson, I mean.'

'Odds on, was he?'

'As I remember it.'

'What are you saying?' Terry asked slowly. 'He was going to win anyway.'

Arthur shrugged. 'So they reckoned.'

But Soldier was more positive. 'He *was* going to win. They just wanted some insurance. Isn't that right, Arthur?'

'That's about it, Soldier.'

Terry stared unbelievingly at them both. 'They thought I couldn't win?'

Arthur looked away unhappily. 'Yeah.'

'Now he tells me.'

'I didn't want to tell you, Tel. I tried to protect you from the knowledge.'

'Thanks, Arthur.'

'Wilson was in on it – of course.' Soldier's voice was bland.

'This gets better all the time.' The bitterness was in his voice now. 'You mean – he wasn't even trying?'

'Look, Tel –' Arthur snapped. 'What the hell does it matter either way? You buggered it up. Then you had your close encounter with the law. It's all history. Who cares now?'

'I bloody care,' said Terry.

'And I reckon Wilson cares,' said Soldier.

'Isn't this great? A couple of has-beens trying to even up a score.'

Terry turned his back on them and began to walk angrily towards the door. En route he took a wild and vicious swipe at the speed-ball.

'He's got the hump,' said Arthur.

'Good,' replied Soldier. 'There's nothing like creating a little adrenalin to make a man fighting mad.'

Terry went straight to the Winchester Club. He was in a blind fury and when Dave suggested an orange juice he told him what to do with it. Quickly Dave poured a pint of lager and put it on the bar in front of Terry.

'So you knew about it as well?' Terry began aggressively.

'Everybody knew – except you. I mean – be fair, Tel. He *was* a bit tasty.'

'Was he?' said Terry, almost to himself.

'Very. Clever, talented, a bit flash – you can't take away his record.'

'And what does that make me – a mug?'

'No. I wouldn't say that, Tel.'

'Then what?'

'Do you really want to know?'

'Might as well.' Terry affected not to care – but it was all too obvious that he cared very deeply indeed.

'It makes you a natural fighter.'

'*What?*'

'That's why they wanted insurance all them years ago. That's the thing about natural fighters – you knock them down and they gets up again. But who needs all that, eh? It's the hell of a way to make a living.'

'I see.' Terry looked abstracted. Then he felt a familiar hand on his shoulder.

'You left without saying goodbye, Terence.' Arthur sounded sure of himself and Terry now knew why. He was accompanied by Soldier, who appeared equally cheerful.

'I'll have the usual, Tel. How about you, Soldier?'

'Just a large brandy.'

'I'll need another four tickets,' said Dave to Arthur. He

turned back to Terry with a grin. 'Some of your fans need 'em. They reckon you'll knock him out.'

'I'm in the chair then?' asked Terry mildly.

'Training expenses,' muttered Arthur.

'Terry,' said Soldier in an admonishing tone, 'that's your last drink until the victory party. Tomorrow we start work – and boy – I do mean work.'

'Sounds great,' said Terry, searching for his wallet.

The training programme nearly killed Terry. Skipping, press-ups, the punch-bag, the speed-ball – Soldier took him through his paces with a punishing determination. There was no let up to the programme and Arthur, watching it, saw Terry gradually and painfully come into a shape and form that was beginning to look promising. His sparring became more positive, more aggressive – and Soldier's well-worn but sound advice was with him all the time. He even began to enjoy the road running and Terry was well ahead of Arthur and Soldier when they followed him in the kerb crawling Jag. Local people began to acknowledge his public progress and stall-holders in the market would cheer him on, occasionally throwing him an apple. Indeed, local interest in Terry's challenge was becoming so great that Arthur, predictably, decided to turn it to his own advantage.

Terry, wearing a new track suit that Arthur had somewhat grudgingly bought him, was standing outside a Greek butcher's in the Fulham Road. Arthur was trying to persuade him to accompany him inside.

'Look, Arthur – leave me out of the sponsorship wheeler-dealing.'

'I need you, Terry. You gotta show yourself.'

'Arthur – I'll show myself in the ring.'

'You have to meet the *people*. You're the local boy. And show a little gratitude – look what I'm doing for you while you're enjoying your training. I'm working on contracts, tickets – getting GBH of the earhole from Soldier.'

'You're the manager, Arthur.'

'And *you're* the product. So come inside the butcher's *now*.'

Reluctantly, Terry followed Arthur inside to find Chris Christodoulides, the butcher, in a state of mild euphoria. He flung his arms round Terry and, having caught him in a warm embrace, said:

'You gotta win, Terry – you really gotta win. For you – I give you the best Scotch sirloin.'

'Great,' said Terry, trying to extricate himself.

Chris let go and rushed over to the counter to cut an enormous steak.

'He can eat two of them,' said Arthur.

'Then two it will be,' he continued to cut. Then he said: 'You get the tickets?'

'Four – that'll be a score each. The best in the house.'

He handed Chris the tickets. He looked at them and exclaimed: 'A score? These say fifteen pounds.'

'Yes,' said Arthur slowly. 'That was a funny business.'

'It was?'

'Arthur's full of jokes,' said Terry. 'Keep us rolling.'

Arthur frowned. 'You ain't gonna believe this Chris, but I had to buy them from a tout. On my landlord's life – it's a sell out.'

'Fancy that,' said Terry.

'It's really caught the public imagination.'

'Of course,' put in Chris naively. 'I want to see my old pal.' He went to the till and took out a few notes. Meanwhile Arthur made good his opportunity.

'You know, Chris – if you had a side of beef, we could have a good picture for the local rag. Terry punching the beef. Remember Rocky?'

'The beef is all cut up,' said Chris. 'How about spring lamb?'

'That'll be fine,' said Arthur.

'You mean I'm gonna punch a little English spring lamb?' complained Terry. 'No way.'

'See – that's your problem, Tel,' Arthur explained patiently.

'What's my problem?'

'You ain't got no killer instinct.'

*

Outside the shop, Arthur decided to part company with Terry. 'You run back to your flat.'

'Thanks. You wouldn't be offering me a lift in the Jag.'

'Training, Terence. What would Soldier say?'

'A lot.'

'Incidentally – I'll have one of those steaks.'

Terry hugged the plastic bag to him.

'They're for me. Training. What would Soldier say?'

'Don't I eat?' Arthur looked stunned.

'As you're selling tickets over the odds – you can buy a turkey and some chippolatas.'

Arthur gave him a wolfish grin. 'You hit 'em on the chin – and I'll hit 'em in the pockets.'

'That's an established tradition,' replied Terry.

'And now I'll trouble you for that steak.'

Reluctantly Terry dipped into the bag.

Brenda was thirty, had seen a bit of life and wear – but she could still turn a few heads. Cool and well preserved, she was sitting at the top of the stairs just outside Terry's flat. Her blonde hair looked as if it had just been styled, and her complexion was as immaculate as ever.

Terry, running up the stairs to the flat and taking pleasure in not being out of breath, paused mid-flight and stared up at her as if he had seen a ghost. For Brenda was not only extremely attractive – she was also the wife of Jackie Wilson and was the very last person he would have expected to see outside the flat.

'Blimey,' was all Terry could think of saying.

'Ain't you gonna invite me in, Tel?'

'I'm – I don't think I should.'

'Scared of what Arthur would say?'

'I was thinking of Jackie.'

'Well, if you're scared of him – God help you!'

'I'm not scared of Jackie.'

'Then – invite me in.'

Slowly Terry walked up the last few steps, unlocked the door and Brenda followed him in.

'I thought you'd be helping out your old man,' said Terry.

'You were always good for a photo at the weigh-in.'

'He doesn't do much training these days.' Brenda gave Terry the benefit of a little pout. 'Don't I get a kiss?'

Terry gave her a perfunctory kiss. Then he said:

'Now, let me guess, Bren. Jackie's got the flu – or is there a deal? Someone fancy a nice big bet?'

'Those days have gone.' She sat down heavily on the sofa. 'Don't I get a drink?'

Terry opened the door of the fridge with a flourish. 'Orange juice, grapefruit juice – or a couple of tea-bags?'

'You really are serious, aren't you?'

'Yeah.'

'He ain't.'

'Oh?'

'He reckons he can lick you anytime. I used to think that too.'

'Did you?'

'Not now.'

'Should be a good fight, then.'

'He could lose an eye.' She was looking at Terry very intently.

'So whose idea is this?' Terry's voice was utterly sceptical. 'Yours or his?'

But she was not to be thrown and Terry tried to avoid her intense look.

'The doctor says he's got a detached retina.'

'Then he shouldn't fight – it's as simple as that.'

'It's not as simple as that –he's got his pride, you know.'

'Don't tell me – tell him.'

'The fight doesn't mean anything – does it? No headlines – just a bit in the local rag.'

'Listen, Brenda, try to get this through you. He doesn't have to fight. Let's call it off. I can fight somebody else.'

'And what's Jackie gonna do?' She sounded indignant. 'He's skint – we've got two kids, a mortgage, debts up to here . . . it's a joke fight.'

'A joke?'

'All I'm saying is – let it *be* a joke fight.' Suddenly the indignation was gone, replaced by a note of fear.

31

'That makes me an all-in wrestler?'

'Well – old ladies like it.'

'Don't be bloody silly, Bren.'

'I'm not *being* bloody silly.'

'You're really serious, aren't you?'

'I'm serious.'

'You want me – to go easy on him.'

'That's all – it's his pride, Tel. That's all I'm asking.'

Terry looked steadily across at Brenda. 'Put it like this, love – I'll consider it.'

Brenda got up. 'I appreciate that, Terry. How about coming out for a quick one?'

'No thanks.'

'Why not?'

'Because I'm training.'

'But –'

'And whether or not I go easy on Jackie – I'm still in training. Get it, Bren?'

'I get it,' she said, walking to the door of the flat. 'No fun till after the fight, then.' Brenda gave a little pout again and Terry said, 'Not ever, love.'

The solicitor's office was tatty – to say the least. Mr Darrow sat at a battlefield of a desk, its top strewn with dog-eared papers, overflowing ashtrays and half-empty coffee cups that looked as if they had been there for days. Darrow himself was almost corpse like – with a deathly pallor and round shoulders that were spotted with dandruff. A rickety looking vintage typewriter stood on a bamboo table and the shelves around the cramped office were overloaded with dusty ledgers and documents.

Arthur and Harry sat themselves down upon two extremely fragile chairs and Arthur gloomily lit up a cigar. Immediately Darrow further depressed him:

'May I trouble you for one of your fine cigars? I seem to have mislaid my own cigar case.'

Arthur silently handed over a cigar.

'How kind. Now – this is the document, Mr Daley?'

In front of him, stagnating in the mess on his desk, were

two pieces of paper. Darrow leant back, drawing reflectively on his cigar. Arthur noticed that he was smoking it as if it was the first cigar he had smoked in years.

'I had suberb chambers in Lincoln's Inn – but I wanted to get back to the people. The grass roots, you understand?'

'The grass roots do the typing?' Arthur looked down censoriously at the ill-typed documents that were littered with mistakes.

'Dear Miss Penrose. Her nimble fingers aren't what they used to be.'

'No – poor dear,' said Harry.

Arthur contented himself with raising his eyebrows.

'I'm bringing in a new word processor next week, gentlemen. I think it will obviate the problem.'

'Does Miss Penrose know how to work one?' asked Arthur.

Mr Darrow smiled sadly. 'I shall be facilitating her work with an assistant, Mr Daley.'

'How kind – isn't the document you've drawn up rather short?'

'Economic, Mr Daley. Economic. I have dispensed with any ramifications with the ground landlord. This is what I call a simple transfer from tenant to tenant –'

'Yes, but – I don't know how to put this, Mr Darrow,' said Arthur.

'Please feel free, Mr Daley.'

'Is it legal, Mr Darrow?'

Darrow looked suitably affronted. 'Well really, Mr Daley – I've worked for some of the largest property companies in the country. I mean – the Duke of Westminster –'

'The *who*?'

'I mean, of course, the *old* Duke.'

'I see.'

'Anyway – you can take this simple lease to your own solicitor . . .'

'That's a laugh,' said Arthur. 'I saw him on the street the other day and asked him how things were. Two days later I get a bill from him.'

Arthur waited in vain for the humorous response, but all Darrow could say was:

'I think I've heard that remark before, Mr Daley.'

'Go on,' said Arthur. 'You can't have done.'

A few minutes later Mr Darrow clearly had nothing else to say and so Arthur and Harry prepared to take their leave.

'You might get that re-typed, Mr Darrow,' said Arthur. 'Just so other people can read it.'

'I don't think I can trespass on any more of Miss Penrose's time,' began Mr Darrow.

Arthur leant on his desk and smiled very sweetly. 'Give Miss Penrose my compliments,' he said, the smile changing to a leer. 'And tell her, I'll make it worth her while.'

'Now lads – I want everything painted white – including the cat – if you can find him. I want brilliant white – and the job finished in a couple of days. How about it?'

There was a mumbled, unenthusiastic response from the three young blacks who were standing in the tatty gloom of Harry's flat. All the furniture had been stacked up against one wall and pots of (bargain) paint had been acquired by Arthur. He had also hired buckets, step ladders and some tarpaulins that looked as if they had come from a butcher.

'A couple of days?' queried one of his newly hired workers. 'That's a bit strong, isn't it?'

Arthur turned on him impatiently. 'We're not talking about David Hicks. Splash it on – white, white and more white. You've got to work like bleeding niggers.'

'Thanks,' said one of the young blacks.

'No disrespect,' said Arthur hastily. 'That's a figure of speech, innit?'

'Is it?' the youngster asked, unappeased.

'You work like three sweaty Irish navvies, all right?'

'That's even worse.'

'Two days anyway,' snapped Arthur, 'wherever you come from.'

Terry's jogging was now a real physical joy to him. He felt tremendously fit and could take most of the exercise in his stride. But to make his training even more interesting, he was now joined by Nicky, from the Job Centre, wearing a very fetching track suit and inevitably trying to match Terry's stride.

'You're not sweating,' she said as they ran laughing up the stairs to Terry's flat.

'That was fun – not running.'

'You must be fit.'

'I *am* fit.'

'Well – I'm not,' Nicky collapsed puffing into an armchair.

'Want to use the shower?'

Nicky looked at him for a moment. Then she said:

'Why not?'

She got up and Terry, with a gracious bow, showed her where the shower was.

'Tea?'

'Great.'

Nicky showered as Terry busied himself with his tea-bags. Then, through the gushing water, Nicky shouted:

'You haven't asked me to come to the fight.'

'Didn't think you'd want to.'

'I've never been to a boxing match.'

'Eh?'

'I said – I've never been to a boxing match.'

Terry filled the kettle. 'There won't be a lot of boxing. It'll be easy for the punters.'

'Why?' Nicky sounded bewildered.

'Because old pros slow down. You can see the punches – and the misses. It's not really for the connoisseur.'

'I'm not exactly a connoisseur.'

'No – but this is memory lane.'

'Then why are you fighting?'

'I don't know,' said Terry. 'It's pathetic!'

'And painful?'

Terry began to make the tea. As he did so, he considered his reply. 'The body punches can be bad, but the blood – well it looks worse than it is. As for the pain – it all depends on whether you lose or win.'

'I see,' said Nicky. 'So – why didn't you ask me to the fight?'

'I just don't think you'd like it. They're – they're special birds who go to fights.'

'Thanks.'

'Look – I don't mean to put you down, Nicky.'

'It's all right.'

'Sure?'

'Yeah – it's all right, Terry.'

Nicky turned the shower on harder. Why wasn't she one of Terry's special birds? Conscious of being clumsy, Terry poured the tea into cups. There was a knock on the door and Terry had a nasty premonition. When he opened the door he found he was right – it was Arthur.

'Relaxing, eh?'

'Well –'

But Arthur pounded on, sounding very elated.

'I woke up this morning and I thought – this is it. 'Er indoors had a dream.'

'Oh yeah?'

'You won.'

'That's nice.'

'Oh – she's well into the premonition game. When I had that unfortunate little business at the Crown Court – 'er indoors had a –'

Just then Nicky entered the room in Terry's dressing gown.

'Oh my Gawd,' said Arthur.

She looked fantastic, glowing with health and her hair still wet from the shower. Arthur rounded on Terry.

'You haven't?'

'Look Arthur –'

'In broad daylight. A few hours before a fight.'

'She's had a shower,' said Terry in a voice that was meant to reassure.

'We were jogging,' said Nicky.

'Is that what they call it now?' said Arthur aghast. He turned back to Terry again. 'You know you've drained your vital fluids, don't you?'

'This is my day off,' said Nicky reasonably.

'*And* giving out your supplementary benefit,' wailed Arthur.

Terry grinned at Nicky.

36

'I forgot to tell you about Arthur.'

'I don't like his innuendoes,' began Nicky.

'Get yourself covered up,' stuttered Arthur, noticing that her dressing gown had opened slightly. 'I'm as liberal as the next man.'

'You're *not*,' replied Nicky.

'But I walk into a well-known bird-bandit's lair and find a comely Richard flaunting her Arris around the gaff –'

'We were just about to have tea,' said Terry.

'Tea? You're supposed to be at a medical check.'

'All right. No sweat.'

'I'm the one whose sweating,' said Arthur.

Terry turned to Nicky. 'Sorry love. I've got to go.'

'Who is he?' asked Nicky.

'My manager,' said Terry. 'His word is law.'

Terry's medical check-up, with background supervision from Arthur, was straightforward. The elderly medical officer began by fumblingly placing a tight band around Terry's arm. He then proceeded to attach it to a blood pressure machine.

'Any illnesses recently?' he quavered.

'No,' replied Terry.

'Eh?' The medical officer was clearly slightly deaf.

'I've been OK,' yelled Terry.

'Anything wrong with your eyes?'

'You tell *me*.'

He stared blearily into Terry's eyes and Terry could smell stale alcohol on his breath.

'They're fine.'

Terry turned to Arthur. 'He's mutton.'

'That doesn't mean to say he's not a good doctor, Terence,' admonished Arthur in a penetrating stage whisper. As he spoke, the M.O. was reading off Terry's blood pressure.

'Well?' asked Terry. 'Am I normal?'

'Excellent – yes, excellent.'

'I say – I'll have a go at that,' said Arthur.

'Eh?'

'Can you take my blood pressure as well?' shouted Arthur.

'If you like,' said the M.O.

'Might as well have a go,' Arthur said to Terry, 'Mine might be higher than yours.' So saying, Arthur took off his jacket and rolled up his sleeves.

'Will you be at the ringside?' Terry asked the M.O. doubtfully.

'Ringside?'

'The role square,' said Terry patiently.

'I'm sorry?'

'The boxing ring,' he yelled.

'I'll be there.' The M.O. turned to Arthur. 'Open your mouth, please.'

Looking worried, Arthur did as he was told.

'Couple of nasty cavities at the back.'

'He's a bleeding dentist,' whispered Terry. 'Now we've got problems.'

'He'll be fine if you get your teeth knocked out – How are mine, mate – are they bad?'

'You should see your dentist.' He took a look at Arthur's blood pressure. 'And your doctor as well.'

Arthur, always a hypochondriac, was instantly alarmed. 'Why?'

'Eh?'

'I said – *why*?' shouted Arthur a shade hysterically.

'I don't want to worry you,' began the M.O.

'But you are,' yelled Arthur. 'I haven't been sleeping that well.'

'Eh?'

'How high is it?'

'High enough.'

'There you are,' said Arthur, turning to Terry. 'I've got it.'

'Got what?'

'The entrepreneur's disease. They drop like flies in Throgmorton Street.'

'You're not under that kind of pressure, Arthur,' said Terry soothingly.

'No? Look at you – lovely and fit. You know why that is?'

'Why is it Arthur?' asked Terry humbly.

'It's because you don't work.'

'I see. And what am I doing tonight?'

'Manual work doesn't count. Churchill had what I've got.' He turned to the M.O. 'Can't you give me some tablets?'

'Eh?'

'Some *tablets*,' Arthur shrieked, but the M.O. merely nodded and smiled for he still could not hear what Arthur was saying.

'Have your usual twelve vodkas instead,' suggested Terry.

'I suppose you think my medical problems are funny?'

'Don't worry, Mr Daley,' said the M.O. 'Nobody ever died from cavities and I'm sure you realise the importance of oral hygiene.'

'What's he on about?' asked Arthur impatiently.

'I think he's saying you'll get by.'

'But it's not my teeth I'm worried about –'

Terry spoke quickly over Arthur's mounting tirade: 'Did you examine Wilson, Doc?'

'Yes – he's fine.'

'Anything wrong with his eyes?'

'They're A1.'

'You sure?'

'Are you questioning my competence, young man?'

'Not at all, sir.' Terry smiled obsequiously and turned back to Arthur. 'If he's the doc – then what's the referee gonna be like?'

'Eric's got everything under control, Terry.'

'I'm sure he has.'

Arthur buttoned up his jacket slowly and went to the door.

'Where are you off to – the Winchester?'

'I'm going for a lie-down.'

'Blimey.'

'In my state of health, Terence, you can't be too careful.'

'I see.'

'And I hope you don't expect too much help in the corner tonight, Tel – not in my state of health.'

Arthur went slowly out, breathing heavily. A few seconds later Terry followed him into the corridor, but Arthur was nowhere to be seen. He must have legged it, thought Terry. But he soon forgot about Arthur – it was bloody weird about

39

the doc not spotting the detached retina in Jackie Wilson's eye. Still, thought Terry, the doc was no good, was he?

Terry lay face down on the table in the tatty dressing room. Soldier, whilst gently massaging his shoulders, was giving him a long, nostalgic lecture on tactics. He was wearing a snappy white tunic with the name TERRY McCANN on the back. With Soldier was an assistant who was clutching a miscellany of Vaseline, swabs and water-bottles, whilst Arthur paced nervously about, his cigar smoke swirling, rather like an expectant father.

'Hot innit?' said Arthur. He looked at Terry's inert form. 'Why isn't he saying anything?' Arthur asked Soldier with a quaver in his voice.

'He's edgy, Arthur – under pressure.'

'Don't say anything about pressure to me,' replied Arthur. 'No one knows how ill I am.' He turned to Terry. 'Is he confident, then?'

'Course he is. I've seen 'em like this before. Mean!'

Terry could stand it no longer and he looked up. Rather than feeling mean, he was both tense and nervous – and the conversation being held over his head was not helping.

'I'm here, you know,' he said. 'I can talk.'

'Len Harvey was the same,' Soldier said to Arthur. 'Calm, but edgy.'

'How the hell can you be calm and edgy at the same time?' asked Terry.

'You see, Arthur,' continued Soldier, 'he's got inner confidence – and he's ready to go out there and do business.'

'Is he?' asked Arthur doubtfully. At that moment one of the stick-on letters that Arthur had supplied for Soldier's tunic fell off, leaving the name 'ERRY McCANN'. Arthur did not consider this was a good omen. Meanwhile, mentally, Terry was going over and over the business of Wilson's eye. Brenda had seemed genuine enough, yet how had the doc missed it? But then the doc was not exactly with it.

'O.K., chaps? I have a capacity crowd for you.'

Eric was standing at the door, beaming and looking hopeful.

'Yeah,' said Arthur sourly. 'I sold most of the tickets, didn't I?'

'I still haven't had the money yet,' returned Eric, his Welsh accent making his voice sound deeply wounded.

'Haven't you?' asked Arthur, fumbling in a number of pockets.

'How's your boy?'

'Fantastic. Let's talk business outside, shall we? I wouldn't want to interrupt Terry's train of thought.'

'What's that?' asked Eric.

'He's thinking mean, aren't you, Terry?'

'Yes, Harry.' Terry had his head down again and Soldier had returned to massaging his shoulders.

Out in the corridor, Arthur somewhat reluctantly handed over the money.

'Any betting around?'

'Plenty. Even Steven. You going to back Terry?'

'I'm not a betting man, but I know he's fit. I also know that Wilson hasn't done much work and he likes a drink.'

'He's got class, though.'

'Has he?'

'But you want to back Terry?'

'Who do I see?'

'Me,' said Eric with a smile.

'I should have known!'

'You're due a monkey on the purse. Why don't you double it?'

'But if Tel loses – I lose everything.'

'Quick, aren't you?'

Arthur stared with active dislike at Eric.

'You've got yourself a bet,' he said.

The atmosphere in the hall was a mixture of cigarette smoke, sweat and stale beer. The audience was predominantly male and Nicky looked around her, feeling self-conscious and jumpy. Then the crowd noise was broken by a tinny fanfare on the P.A. system and Terry jogged into the arena, wearing a hooded dressing gown and accompanied by Soldier and his assistant. Arthur walked regally a few paces behind them,

41

rather as if he were the star attraction himself.

As Terry ran towards the ring he could make out a number of familiar faces – Detective Constable Rycott, Chris the Greek butcher, Dave and others. But rather than reassuring him, they merely made him feel uneasy. As Terry climbed into the ring he saw Brenda sitting in the front row and his uneasiness increased. That eye – that bloody eye. Wilson was already there when he arrived and as Terry stripped off his gown and began to limber up, a buxom girl in the ring was strutting around with a placard indicating the number of rounds in the fight.

'Who's the bird?' Terry asked.

'Eric's cousin – she goes to the loser,' Arthur replied seriously.

'What's up, Arthur?'

'I'm ill.'

'You're so reassuring, aren't you?'

'You don't know what kind of strain I'm under, Tel.'

'Anyone would think you were going into the ring.'

'I feel as if I am.'

Then the M.C. stepped into the middle of the ring and began to announce the fight.

'Ladies and Gentlemen. We now come to the main event in tonight's programme. A middleweight bout of ten rounds introducing the popular Fulham Typhoon – Terry McCann.'

There was a burst of applause and through it Terry said to Arthur: 'That was your idea, wasn't it?'

'What?'

'Typhoon – The Fulham Typhoon.'

'It's an image, isn't it?' Arthur replied vaguely, his hand shaking on his cigar.

'Pull yourself together, Arthur.'

'I'm ill, Tel. Very ill.'

'You'll be all right.'

'And one of the greats,' continued the M.C. 'Ex-middleweight Champion of Britain and the Commonwealth – Jackie Wilson. And your referee, Ladies and Gentlemen, is Bernie Sandilands.' There was full applause, the M.C. left the ring and the referee called Terry and Jackie to the middle. In the audience, Detective Constable Rycott turned to a plain-clothed colleague and whispered:

'I hope you've got your notebook, my son. There's plenty of faces on the wanted list, here.' He stared round the audience. 'I mean – look over there – that's Archie Harris – he should be in Parkhurst, shouldn't he?'

Meanwhile, Soldier was saying to Terry, 'We've got time, Terry. Plenty of time – so feel him out.'

But Arthur was not having any. 'Knock him out, Terry. Soon as you can – then we can go home early.'

Terry attempting to ignore Arthur, suddenly caught Nicky's eye and grinned. She smiled hesitantly back and then the bell went for the first round. Immediately, Terry was up on his toes and moving well. Wilson gave him a few tentative jabs, but they were well out of reach. Then, Wilson tried a right, but Terry was ducking and moving away, easily avoiding the blow. The audience were bored and began to catcall, suspecting they were going to witness a tame fight. But they were cheered by a flurry of punches from Terry and the sight of Wilson retreating fast. Terry pursued him to the corner where Wilson clinched and held on desperately.

'Go on, my son,' shouted Arthur, his eyes bulging and his cigar dead in his mouth.

Getting out of the clinch, Wilson also managed to evade Terry. Over-anxious, Terry tried to get in with a badly-calculated punch, but he failed to make contact. The fans groaned and the bell resounded.

'Don't let him sit down,' said Arthur scrambling into the ring. 'He'll go to sleep.'

'All right, Arthur,' said Soldier, looking disappointed.

'Get out,' said Terry.

'But what's going on?' asked Arthur as Terry sat down on his stool.

'He don't want to fight.'

'That's no reason for you not to. Come on – I've got money on this.'

'On who?'

'I've got a monkey on the Fulham Typhoon. So let's get busy.' Arthur turned desperately to Soldier. 'Go on – tell him about Tommy Farr and Len Harvey again.'

'Relax, Arthur. Now Tel, just settle down. You've got nothing to beat.'

The girl with the placard bounced into the ring and announced Round Two as Soldier said, 'Be first, son.'

'Yeah,' said Arthur. 'Get in there. And be quick.'

'Arthur,' Terry said as the bell went, 'Why don't you drop off?'

Terry was jabbing away until Wilson forced him into a clinch. Leaning on Terry's shoulder, he whispered:

'Take it easy – I'm knackered. I've got a dodgy eye.'

'Lie down, then.'

'No talking there,' shouted the referee.

Wilson twisted round Terry – and went on whispering, out of the referee's earshot.

'Don't hit me eye.'

'Then what?'

'Body shots – they're O.K.'

'Lie down – I've told you once.'

'Make it good then.'

The referee broke them apart and as he did so, Terry glanced towards Brenda. She seemed very anxious. Looking hard, Terry moved in with a series of body jabs and Wilson winced. But as he did so, Terry suddenly, instinctively knew he had been conned. Terry's face was open and Wilson was suddenly raining punches to his head. They were good – and Wilson was showing all the form and pace of a former champion. The crowd began to roar and with a right cross Terry was thrown back on the canvas. The referee began to count as blood gushed from Terry's eye but, somehow, he managed to heave himself off the ropes.

Wilson then came in for the kill with a fierce combination of punches and the crowd roared again. Nicky buried her face in her hands – and so did Arthur. Soldier stared woodenly at Terry as he pawed at the ropes again.

'Blimey,' muttered Terry as he just beat the count. For a moment he mistily caught Brenda's expression. There was a mixture of triumph and pain on her face. Terry then found himself being led to his corner by the referee and Wilson continued to prance around the middle of the ring, giving a victory salute to the cheering crowd. His two corner-men were already embracing him.

'He conned me,' said Terry muzzily to Arthur and Soldier. 'What round is it?'

'It's over, son,' replied Soldier.

'What?'

'I said, it's –'

But Terry was away from him, rushing at Wilson, whose arm the referee had not yet raised.

'My Gawd,' said Arthur, putting his hands over his eyes again.

Wiping the blood from his face, Terry pushed the referee away and was on to Wilson. His two corner-men tried to whisk him away, but Terry knocked one of them over. The other tried to swing a punch but to no avail, for Terry gave him a backhander and he went sprawling onto the canvas. Wilson squared up to Terry and in a second they were at it, toe to toe, trading punch for punch. The referee tried ineffectively to stop them as Eric shouted at him:

'Don't bloody stop 'em, Bernie. This is the last fight of the night!'

As Terry and Wilson slugged it out, the crowd were on their feet and Arthur gradually took his hands away from his eyes. He could see Dave, Chris and even Detective Constable Rycott shouting for Terry. Nicky stared ahead, her eyes glazed and, in another part of the hall, Brenda watched transfixed.

Gradually, Terry's right-hand blows and his passionate anger told on Wilson, who began to go down under the massive attack. Then, after a beautiful right and left from Terry, he hit the deck, with the crowd going crazy and Soldier yelling to Arthur: 'It's a classic fight, Arthur. A fight for history!'

But Terry did not acknowledge the adulation of the cheering. Instead, he turned away, climbed out of the ring and shouldered his way through the crowd to the dressing room. Arthur, meanwhile, having recovered his composure, went after an exultant Eric.

'Oh Taff –'

'Yes, Arthur?'

'You owe me money.'

'You reckon?'

'He won, didn't he?'

'That's a debatable point. The ref stopped it.'

'You can tell that to Jackie Wilson. We ain't exactly talking about the Queensberry Rules, are we?'

'You know what I'm going to do, Arthur?' said Eric triumphantly.

'No,' said Arthur suspiciously.

'That fight was like one of the fights my Da used to talk about. You've got a result, Arthur – and I don't want you ever to say that I'm not generous.'

'You mean –' Arthur's smile was beginning.

'You won.'

'You're a gentleman, Eric,' said Arthur, pumping his hand.

Soldier was swabbing at Terry's eye in the dressing room.

'I'm proud of you, son.'

'It was a street fight,' said Terry.

'Most fights start there.'

Arthur, clutching a wad of notes, entered cheerfully with the deaf M.O. in tow.

'Good on yer, Terry.'

'Thanks, Arthur.'

'We're on next month.'

'No, we're not.'

'Eh?' Arthur looked flabbergasted. 'Look Tel – don't you understand? You punch-drunk or something? You've got a new career. You're the people's champion.'

'Shut up, Arthur.'

'I beg your pardon, Terence. I hope all this hasn't gone to your head.'

'I had a career,' said Terry firmly, 'seven years ago. So forget it.' He looked up at the M.O. vaguely advancing towards him. 'And get him out before he has my teeth.'

'I was terrified,' said Nicky when Terry had showered and changed.

'I wasn't too happy at one point,' said Terry.

'I don't like boxing.'

'I didn't think you would.'

'You going on with it?'

'Arthur wants me to.'

'But –'

'I'm not going to do it.'

She smiled with relief. 'What are you going to do instead? Come back to the Job Centre.'

'I've got a job.'

'What's that?'

'Looking after Arthur.'

'Is that a job?'

'Not much of one.'

'Then, why not change it?'

'I've got used to it.'

'You're in a rut.'

'I know. Tell you what – let's go somewhere.'

'Where to?'

'How about my place?'

Next day, Arthur parked his car outside Harry's flat. Terry, wearing dark glasses, was sitting with Nicky in the back. Arthur got out, went round to the boot and pulled out an awful framed reproduction of 'The Stag at Bay'.

'Nice, isn't it?' he said as he showed it to Terry through the car window.

'I thought you was taking us out to lunch?'

'I will in a minute. Just hang about – I'm refurbishing one of my properties.'

Holding the picture, Arthur walked towards the flats whilst Nicky took off Terry's dark glasses and examined the bruise round his eye.

'If you had a real job – you could claim industrial compensation.'

'From Arthur?'

'Why not?'

'You don't know Arthur,' said Terry.

Nicky sighed, 'I think I'm beginning to,' she said.

Once on the landing, Arthur was surprised to find the door of Harry's flat open. Inside, he could see that the flat had been painted but he could also see three suitcases in the middle of the floor. Stepping inside, Arthur gazed incredulously at them until a shrewish-looking woman in her mid-forties came out of the bedroom. She stared indignantly at Arthur.

'Who the hell are you?'

'I might ask you the same, madam,' said Arthur pompously. 'I happen to own this apartment.'

'Do you now! So you're a squatter, are you?'

'Certainly not.'

'*I* live here.'

Light dawned in Arthur's eyes. 'I see – you're Harry's wife.'

'What if I am?'

'You've been blown out, love.'

'And what's that meant to mean?'

'If you will go off with double-glazing men and desert the domestic home. No wonder Harry's sold the gaff.'

'Sold? This is a council flat.'

'You must realise, madam, that I'm the legal tenant of this – what did you say?'

'I said – this is a council flat.'

'My Gawd.'

'Now – get out.'

But Arthur did not move. Instead he simply stood there, his mouth opening and shutting without a sound emerging.

'Are you going – or shall I call the police?'

In a trance, Arthur went.

Very slowly, as if he was an old man, Arthur opened the car door.

'What's the matter?' asked Terry.

'I'm ill.'

'Yeah – but aren't you still taking us out for lunch – to celebrate?'

'Celebrate what?'
'And you're gonna pick up the tab?'
'You're taking advantage of a sick man.'
'You can be sick after lunch, Arthur,' said Terry.

PART TWO

Arthur took a long time getting over Harry's con. He talked about it incessantly and both Terry and Dave took a pasting as they tried to commiserate with him.

'You're too trusting, Arthur,' said Dave one night at the Winchester and Terry agreed.

'You should have sussed it out more, Arthur.'

'You're a couple of Jim's comforters, aren't you?'

'Eh?'

'Who is Jim?'

'You don't seem to understand – either of you – that I'm a decent kind of bloke. I don't *expect* to be conned. I'm a respectable businessman.'

'You're a schmuck,' said Terry.

'Thank you, Terence. After all I've done for you – rescuing you from the audio-typists and swinging ropes, giving you a career – and then having you throw it all up. And now you call me a schmuck!'

'You should have grabbed your opportunity, Arthur,' said Dave.

'What opportunity?'

'The one Harry's wife gave you,' continued Dave. 'You should have given her a little something to remember you with. After all – you were alone in the flat?'

'You seem to forget I have 'er indoors.'

'That's never stopped you,' put in Terry.

'To decorate a council flat,' said Arthur. 'All that paint, that stripper, those brushes –'

'What stripper?' asked Terry. 'You didn't say you laid on one for the boys. I'd have given you a hand if you'd said.'

'Another vodka,' cried Arthur piteously.

'I can't put much more on the slate, Arthur. You're well over the limit.'

'Then buy me a vodka,' cried Arthur. 'Help me in my hour of need.'

'We've all been done,' said Terry. 'Lay off it for a bit, Arthur.'

'Been done? When've you been done?'

'I was done when I met you, Arthur,' replied Terry quietly.

Dave grinned. 'Cheer up, Arthur. Just think how lucky you are.'

'Lucky?'

'Yeah – Harry could've sold you the whole block.'

To cheer himself up, Arthur went to a masonic dinner the next night. Returning home by mini-cab and in a highly drunken condition, Arthur bumped into an old friend. He limped out of the shadows, a man in his late thirties who was handsome in a brutish sort of way.

'Hallo, Arthur.'

'Who the hell –' Arthur blundered about on the pavement, basically trying to stand up.

'It's Billy.'

'Blimey – what are you doing lurking?' Arthur swayed in front of him. 'You all right, Billy – oh dear, oh dear – what have you done?'

Arthur had finally noticed that there was a very nasty swelling on Billy's face.

'I need some help, Arthur.'

'You look as if you could use some.'

'Like now.'

'Come and have a nice drink.'

'I need a lift – can you drive me somewhere?' Billy's voice was hoarse with fatigue.

'Can't in my state, old son,' replied Arthur shakily. 'I'm plastered – been to a function – can't cope with a car.'

'Know anyone who can?'

'Come in and tell me all about it.'

'I need a ride *now*, Arthur. I've done me leg in.'

Arthur grasped Billy's shoulder in a drunken embrace. 'Are we friends, Billy?'

'We certainly are, Arthur.'

'Really good mates?'

'You can bet your life on it.'

'Then I will get you a ride, my son – if necessary to the very ends of the earth.' He began to guide Billy erratically down the street.

'Where are we going, Arthur?'

'We? Where are *we* going?'

'Yes Arthur – where are we going?' There was a dangerous edge to Billy's voice, but Arthur was too drunk to detect it.

'We're goin' to an ole friend. A very ole friend.'

'And he'll help me?'

'He helps everyone,' said Arthur, 'even me.'

Terry was in bed with Nicky when Arthur called. He sat bolt upright in bed as Arthur lurched around on the landing. Then Terry heard the penetrating stage whisper.

'Terry – open up.'

'I'm asleep.'

Nicky clapped a hand over her mouth as she felt an overpowering urge to giggle.

'It's important, Terry.'

Terry climbed out of bed, opened the front door and pushed Arthur back onto the landing.

'Yeah.'

'You know Billy Gilpin?'

'You wake me up for introductions?'

'Billy needs a favour.'

'Does he?'

'You gonna let us in?'

'I'd rather we talked here.'

'That's not very social, Tel.'

'I'm not a very social person.'

'Look – Terry – I've said this is important.' The drink in Arthur made him slightly belligerent and Terry raised his eyebrows. Then, suddenly, he gave in and reluctantly led them into the kitchen.

'Well?'

'Any coffee, Tel?'

'Not at this time of night, Arthur. Come on – spill it.'

'I said to Billy that there's one bloke I know who wouldn't let anyone down –' Arthur began conversationally.

'Look,' said Terry, finally coming clean. 'I've got a bird in there.'

'Nicky?'

'It doesn't matter who she is.'

'She's a girl after me own heart.'

'Let's get on with it, Arthur,' said Billy, the edge returning to his voice.

'I'll explain it all to Nicky,' Arthur lurched towards the bedroom door and Terry grabbed him just in time.

'Please, Arthur.'

'I'm sorry, Terry,' said Billy. 'I'm desperate for this favour.'

Then the interruption came.

'Coffee anyone?' Nicky appeared from the bedroom.

'Don't mind if I do, Nicky,' said Arthur. 'You really are the sweetest little –'

'Hang on,' said Terry.

'What's up?' she asked.

'I'm going out,' said Terry.

'Thanks, pal,' put in Billy.

'For a while.'

'You are, are you?' Nicky's good humour vanished.

'I won't be long.'

'It's always the same – when that man comes –' She pointed angrily at Arthur. 'That awful man.'

'Nicky,' began Arthur. 'Darling girl –'

'Shut up, Arthur,' said Terry.

'You stay out of this,' replied Arthur. 'I can –'

'The only person who's staying out is me,' snapped Nicky.

'Wait a minute –' pleaded Terry.

'No. I'm always waiting. I'm going to dress.'

'Do you want some help?' sniggered Arthur as she slammed the kitchen door.

'Your charm,' said Terry slowly. 'It always wins through in the end, doesn't it?'

Terry drove Billy in his elderly Ford. For a while they said nothing and Terry pulled out onto the Brighton road and began to drive at a considerable rate of knots.

'Not so fast,' said Billy. 'We don't want to get a pull.'

Terry slowed down. 'You're right – this motor ain't been MOT'd for two years.'

Billy was uneasily silent again. Then he said: 'No music?'

'No music.'

'I like a number called Friends.'

'Don't know it.' Terry sounded as if he wanted to make as little social contact with Billy as possible.

'It's true though.'

'What is?'

'Friends – I won't forget this, Terry.'

'No?'

'A friend is a guy you can go to in the middle of the night – and he'll help you. No questions – nothin'.'

'You went to Arthur.'

'He took me to you.'

'That's Arthur's friendship all over.'

There was a long pause. Then Billy said: 'You haven't asked, have you?'

'Asked what?'

'What happened to Billy's pretty face.'

'I don't want to know.'

'And his leg?'

'I told you – I don't want to know.'

'Arthur's got an address – I'll see you're looked after.'

'I thought it was all down to friendship.'

'And it is. But there's no harm in giving your friends a drink, is there? People don't understand that – people I've known for years. And the filth – no way would they believe my story.'

'I don't want to hear it, Billy.'

He speeded up the Ford, but Billy said quickly: 'For Christ's sake Terry – slow down.'

Terry slowed down and Billy relaxed again. 'It's a beautiful night, isn't it?'

'Mm.'

'We turn off before Brighton.'

'O.K.'

'I've forgotten me tablets.'

'Well, I ain't going back for 'em.'

'They put me on tablets, you know. Me – a champagne man. I love the bubbly – I can dance on it all night. But I get down, depressed like – that's why they put me on the tablets. They thought I might top meself.'

Terry shot Billy an appraising glance but Billy was

vacantly staring at the countryside around them. Then he said, 'Take the next turning.'

Terry did as he was told.

'Sorry about that bird of yours.'

'That's all right – it was coming.'

'What does she do?'

'Works in a Job Centre.'

'Useful.'

'Maybe.'

'I used to pull little girls like that. Moved on now, you know.'

'Oh yeah.'

'You gotta move on – I only go for the class. Strictly jet set now.'

'Well I'm still hanging around with the off-peak stand-by lot.'

But Billy was not listening. 'I was in the papers three times last month. They made me a celebrity in the gossip columns and just because of the company I was keeping.'

'I hope you're not in them tomorrow.'

'O.K.' said Billy with a sudden brusqueness. 'Next right and you'll find a little hotel at the top of the hill.'

A few minutes later, they stopped outside a shuttered building standing on top of a small hill. The night was clear and still.

'You're gonna check in at this time of night with no bags?' queried Terry. He leant across Billy to open the door for him.

'Without friends,' said Billy, 'it's not worth living.'

'You got friends here?'

'Another mate.'

'You're a lucky man.'

'That's something I always remember, Tel. How lucky I am.'

Billy got out of the car and walked over to the door of the hotel. He knocked at it gently and as Terry drove away, he could see a light switched on at an upstairs window.

The roads were empty on the way back to London and Terry drove slowly, mulling over the events of the night. There was something about his own involvement in Billy's journey that made Terry uneasy. Obviously his very appearance had underlined he had been up to no good – but it wasn't just that. It was something else that Terry could not pin down.

Arriving back at his flat, Terry climbed wearily out of the car and yawningly struggled up the stairs. He searched in his pockets for the key to the front door, cursing as he did so. What he wanted was not just a kip, but Nicky as well – two important parts of his life that Arthur had deprived him of. At last Terry found his key and he opened the door of the flat slowly. As he crossed the threshold, he had a premonition that something unpleasant was about to happen – and when he opened the sitting room door, he discovered what it was. Two young men were sitting there, one examining Terry's record collection, the other flicking through a magazine. Without asking, Terry knew they were plain clothed policemen.

'Terence McCann?' said the man on the sofa, flicking out a warrant card.

'I'd never have guessed who you were without seeing that.'

'You must have seen quite a few in your time,' said the other detective, putting down a record.

'You've no right breaking in here.'

'Breaking in? We were kindly allowed access to the premises by your associate.'

One word lit itself angrily in Terry's mind – Arthur.

'Where is he?'

'Here I am, Tel.'

Arthur came in from the bathroom, looking pale and ill. His collar was open and his black tie dangled hopelessly. He flopped into a chair and groaned.

'I don't think your friend's very well,' said one of the detectives.

'I was having a kip, Terry,' said Arthur, 'when the front door –'

'All right, Arthur,' said Terry quietly.

'Shall we take a ride?' The detective smiled up at Terry.

'What happens if I say no?'

'Well,' the detective looked at his colleague, 'Steve here

will jump on you and I'll say you assaulted him and you'll be remanded in custody . . . which would be rather silly really because all we want to do is to have a talk with you. So what's it going to be?'

'Since you put it so nicely – I'd love to come.'

'Say bye-bye to your obliging friend.'

'Yes,' said Terry reflectively. 'You've got to have friends, haven't you? Bye-bye, Arthur.'

At the police station, Terry was interviewed by an old acquaintance – the middle-aged, patient and cynical Detective Inspector Barrett. He sat opposite Terry, flanked by another, younger detective.

'You see, Terry,' said Barrett, 'everywhere I go I see dirt – everywhere I listen I hear lies. But I've always had a kind of faith in you. No trouble for five years now.'

'That's right.'

'I thought you were a walking testimony to the reformative powers of the British penal system. And then – just like that – you're running a mini-cab service for nasty villains like Billy Gilpin.'

'I gave him a lift. That's no crime – is it?'

'It all depends, Terry. I mean – two villains walk out of a shop with a string of pearls that don't belong to 'em – and someone gives 'em a lift. That's a crime, isn't it?'

Terry said nothing.

'Eh?'

'It's a crime.'

'And what about attempted murder, then? That a crime in your book?'

'Yeah.'

'And aiding and abetting the escape of a man wanted for murder?'

'I dunno what he did,' said Terry defensively.

'But I just told you what he did.'

Terry stared down at the table.

'Then he didn't mention it.'

'What did he talk about?'

'He didn't say much. He talked about friends.'

'Which friends?'

'He didn't say. He said he was lucky to have 'em.'

'What about Lord Ingram?'

'Who?'

'Did he mention that name?'

'No – what is it – a boozer?'

'He's the feller Billy tried to murder.'

'Well – if he did, he never mentioned it.'

Barrett leant across the table and spoke softly to Terry. 'Listen Terry. I'm not asking you to be a super-grass. But I *am* advising you to have a slightly more co-operative attitude. You see – if there's attempted murder on my patch I get something – see. I either get the guy who did it – or the guy who helped him get away.' He paused, sat back and spoke in a louder voice: 'Am I coming through to you loud and clear?'

'I'm with you,' said Terry.

'So, I'd like you to go and have a little think.'

'At home?'

'No, Terry – in a cell. On your ownio.'

Terry lay miserably on the lower bunk of the cell. He looked around, registering again the claustrophobia of a place that he had hoped he would never see again. A feeling of desolation swept over him. He would never be allowed to put it all behind him – not in the end.

Suddenly the door opened and a thick-set man was shown in to the confined space. He glanced round the cell quickly and then his eyes rested on Terry. When he spoke it was with a Northern accent and a very ingratiating manner, but beneath all this, Terry detected a basic toughness.

'The name's Whaley. Colin Whaley.'

'Terry McCann.'

'I've got the top one, then.'

'Looks like it.'

'That's O.K. by me.' He gave Terry a quick, insincere smile. 'I've had plenty of practice anyway.' Whaley hauled himself up to the top bunk. 'Just done a five in Durham,' he continued. 'Only out two weeks, when the bastards grabbed me. They don't give you a chance down here.' He paused as if to allow Terry to reply, but received no response. Terry was playing it cool, determined to give nothing away. 'Attempted robbery, they say. And they gave me a right kicking on the way down. Stuff the bastards – that's what I say. Stuff 'em.' He leant over the bunk to take a good look at Terry. 'What you in for, then?'

'Not a lot.'

Whaley continued, undeterred by Terry's reticence. 'I've been everywhere you know. Maidenhead, Hull – I was even up in Peterhead. I did pottery and carpet weaving up there.'

'They nicked you for it?'

'I did that inside. Occupational therapy, they called it.' He leant over again to take another look at Terry. 'Don't say much, do yer.'

'I don't stand much of a chance with you up there.'

'Don't mind me. I'm just the outgoing type. I like getting on with people.'

'I've already sussed that out.'

'Straight I am.' He swung down off the bunk. 'You seem a bit worried. Depressed like.'

Terry gave him a cynical glance. 'Don't worry about it.'

'Why not?'

'Because you might become me best pal.'

'So –'

'In a fit of depression and remorse I tell you my life story.'

'Yeah. If it helps.'

'And what I done and how I did it and the first I learn of it is when you're in the box swearing my life away.'

'You got it all wrong. I'm just trying to be a friend.'

'I've had enough friends for one day.'

'But –'

'OK?'

Terry turned over and attempted, with difficulty, to find himself a comfortable sleeping position. Disappointed, Whaley stared down at him and then, with a shrug, levered himself up onto the top bunk again.

'You don't talk in your sleep an' all do you?' Terry said.

*

The next morning, they let Terry go. He felt relieved but also exhausted and somehow institutionalised again – despite the shortness of his stay. As he walked angrily down the corridor of the police station, Barrett passed him.

'Ah, Terry – you won't go nipping off to Majorca, will you? We may want you to come in again.'

Not trusting himself to say anything, Terry simply scowled and walked on. His mood was not improved by meeting Arthur as he left the police station. Arthur was still wearing his dinner-suit, was unshaved and looked distinctly seedy.

'You've got me to thank for getting you out of there,' said Arthur.

'I got you to thank for getting me *in* there.'

'Nice innit – me walking about at this time of day looking like this. Think of my position.'

'They'll think you've been in for a fitting.'

'Fit up more like it. Think of the dinners I've been to with some of these people. I mean – a D.I., who shall be nameless, has me to thank for giving him a deep-freeze at a give-away price. A real steal!'

'I'm sure that was just what it was, Arthur.'

'That's beside the point, Terry.'

Arthur tried to hail a cab but was swiftly beaten by an Arab.

'They're as bad, an' all. If you ain't got a kaftan – you ain't got no chance. I'll tell you –'

But Terry cut firmly across Arthur's flow. 'What about Billy?'

'You never know with him. Could be doing a bit of cross-channel swimming.'

'He talked about topping himself when I was driving him.'

'Well, I hope he made a phone call about our loot before he done it.'

'You're a real friend to Billy, aren't you, Arthur? No wonder he values his friends so highly.'

'So, I'll cry a little,' returned Arthur truculently. 'But I still want the loot.'

'I'm going home.'

'No, you're not, Terry.'

'Arthur – I'm knackered.'

'You'll feel much better after a quiet sauna and a change of attire.'

'Why?'

'Because we have to visit Lady Ingram.'

'Who?'

'Lady Anne Clare Ingram. Who is –'

'– the missus of the feller Billy tried to murder.'

'That's their own personal affair, Terence.'

'So – what's ours?'

'Our wages. That's something else – innit?'

'Is it?'

'Since when have you grown cold on loot – specially after all the aggravation you've had?'

'I'm going home.'

'And then?'

'I'll meet yer.'

'Well done, Terry. That's my boy.'

'But Arthur –'

'Yes?'

'If I ever go back inside, I'm holding you personally responsible.'

'You – inside?'

'Yeah. I caught the smell of it again. Know what I mean?'

'Sorry, Tel. I wouldn't.'

'You will, Arthur. One day – you will.'

The traffic in Terry's flat was getting very heavy. Last night he had met the filth in his front room. Now he met the heavies on the landing.

A young well-dressed man was leaning against the door and another, equally well-dressed, but bigger and harder-looking, was standing a few feet away.

'Terence McCann?'

'Why am I so popular?'

'I don't know, Terry. P'raps you aren't. Not doing a runner, are you?'

'Who the hell *are* you?'

'We're not the old Bill.'

'Hard to tell, these days.'

'We only want to have a talk.'

'That's what the old Bill said. Last time it lasted too long.'

'But Bobby Altman gets to the point so much more quickly than the filth.'

'Who's Altman?'

'Friend of Billy Gilpin's.'

'Another *friend*?'

'Yeah – a big one.'

'That word's always cropping up.'

'Eh?'

'Friend. Billy was really into friends, wasn't he?'

But they were both advancing down the stairs.

'Come on, Terry,' said the well-built one. Terry turned wearily back down the stairs.

Bobby Altman believed in keeping himself fit and today was no exception. For his normal jog across Hampstead Heath Bobby, who was touching fifty and had dragged himself from the East End to the Heights, wore a well-cut track suit and highly expensive running shoes. As he came into view, a Ford Granada pulled up, disgorging Terry and his two new-found friends. On the pavement was another young man, who was standing opposite a neo-Georgian mansion that screamed money from every well turned brick.

'How much has he done?' asked one of Terry's captors.

'On his fourth mile.'

Terry noticed there was a Rolls Royce parked outside the garage and as Altman came jogging up, one of his underlings passed him a towel. As he wiped away the sweat, Altman gave Terry a shrewd, slightly patronising look. Then he draped the towel round his neck, took his own pulse and said casually to Terry:

'Do a bit of jogging?'

'Now and again.'

'Tennis, squash, badminton?'

'No.'

'Work out at the gym?'

'Sometimes.'

'I remember you, Terry McCann.'

'Oh?'

'Saw your fight.'

'Against Wilson?'

'No – first time round.'

'Oh – I see.'

'You were badly handled.'

'Yeah.'

'But you've gone a long way since then.'

'Maybe.'

'Now you're an even bigger mug.'

The other three men came very close to Terry as Altman said: 'Do come in.' He indicated the house with the Rolls outside. Terry hesitated. 'Please,' said Altman. 'Any friend of Billy's is a friend of mine.'

'You work for Arthur Daley?'

'Sort of.'

Altman was in the shower and Terry was standing in a room that had been expertly converted into a gym. New, gleaming equipment invited maximum exertion and a statue of Adonis suggested the ideal.

'You know what he is?'

Terry thought hard. To Altman, none of the things that Arthur was could be considered complimentary. But Altman did not wait for an answer.

'Arthur is a financial midget.'

Terry did not reply and Altman, still in the shower, shouted out, 'Try the speed-ball, Terry.'

'I'm O.K., thanks.'

'He said to try it,' put in one of Altman's heavies. Terry slowly crossed to the speed-ball and began to hammer it. The heavies watched, impressed despite themselves for Terry was both fast and accurate. He went into a very fancy two-handed tattoo on the ball and Altman emerged from the shower to watch him, wrapping himself in a bath-robe, handed to him by one of his acolytes. Terry concluded his work out with a hefty right hander that almost parted the ball from its moorings. He then turned to face Altman who was drinking a large tumblerful of orange juice. He then sat himself down on a swivel chair and grandiosely motioned to Terry to sit down on one opposite him.

Altman took his own pulse again. 'I run for miles. I take a shower. I sit down and my pulse is normal again.'

'Lucky you,' said Terry.

'I have a very slow heart-beat – fifty-six a minute. Athletes half my age would give anything for a pulse rate like that. Now, Terry, all this means that I'm a very calm and rational man. The only time that my pulse rate quickens is when I talk about money. And the only time it starts to race is when I talk about money that's been stolen from me.'

'What money?'

'Billy Gilpin stole my money and you helped him get away.'

'I didn't know what he'd been doing.'

'And now they tell me he's dead.'

'Dead?' Terry's voice registered sudden alarm.

'Or so I hear. But I don't know whether to believe it or not.'

'Did the buzz say how he died?'

'They say he walked into the water.'

'And you reckon it's not true?'

'I say it's bullshit. With seventy grand Billy Gilpin could walk *on* the water.'

'Look – all I did was to give him a lift.'

'So what does that make you?' asked Altman menacingly.

'It makes me the guy who gave him a lift – that's all.'

'No, Terry. It makes you an accomplice. It makes you the man who helped steal money from *me*.'

'Look –'

Altman jumped up, the anger etched hard on his face.

'I'm excited now, Terry. I'm angry too – and what happens when I'm angry? My heart starts racing.'

He began to walk round Terry. 'Heard of the Ayatollah?'

'Yeah.'

'I'm a fan of his.'

'He needs a few.'

'What happens? You steal in his country and he cuts your

hand off. So, if you steal from *me* – then don't worry about referendums, don't worry about free votes in the House of Commons, don't worry about anything like that.' He continued to pace around Terry and then he stopped, leaning over to within an inch of his face. 'If you steal from me – I bring back capital punishment.'

'I could plead diminished responsibility.'

'And what's that supposed to mean?' asked Altman, looking sarcastically round at his three heavies.

'That I don't know nothing.'

'I see. You didn't even wonder what was in his little Gucci briefcase?'

'He didn't have a case.'

Terry sounded so positive that Altman paused for a minute and Terry knew that he was wondering, for the first time, whether or not he was on the level.

'So his pockets were bulging?' asked Altman.

'No – but his eye was bulging. And he had a dodgy leg.'

'You're St John's Ambulance, are you? An overgrown boy scout? Anybody's a bit out of sorts and you're the first to give them a helping hand. He's a pal, is he?'

'I never met him before.'

Altman seemed genuinely surprised as he once more turned to his acolytes. 'You believe that, chaps? This guy's terrific. He's the last of the English gents.'

'I just did a favour.'

'That's nice, isn't it? A nice favour – and maybe I'll even believe you.' Altman stared very hard at Terry. 'Now you're in my house and you've seen the bricks and mortar. Right?'

Terry nodded.

'You've seen this gym and you've probably noticed it's bigger and better than your living room. I've got a lot of staff and I spend a lot of money. Look at my lads – well dressed with a nice wedge in their pockets. Look at Stuart now. When he came down from Scotland he had 50p in his sporran. Now he's got a gold Dupont lighter and the guy doesn't even smoke.'

Terry watched Altman's face. He seemed to be calming down slightly and maybe he was going to be ready to strike some kind of deal. But *what* kind of deal?

'You know what a bearer bond is?'

'No.'

'Course you don't – they're like money. You take 'em to a bank and they pay you out – face value. We've been doing that, see, France, Germany, Switzerland . . . Never mind how we got 'em. We've been selling 'em, right?'

Again Terry nodded, his mind furiously trying to get one ahead of Altman – and failing.

'You need a bit of front for what I'm doing – that's why pretty Billy was on the firm. Then – temptation falls in the lad's path.'

'You sure?'

'I'm sure. And if he didn't have the money on him when he was with you – somebody's looking after it for him. That's logical.'

'Yeah.'

'How did he come to you, Tel?'

Terry hesitated.

'Come on.'

He glanced at the three heavies who looked as if they might like to see some action at any minute.

'Arthur brought him.'

'Now that figures. You don't need a pocket calculator for that.' He poured himself out some more orange juice and almost drained the glass. 'Terry – I want you to go and tell Arthur that I want my money.'

'I'm not sure he can help you – any more than I can.'

'Tell him if I don't get it – he's a dead man.'

Altman wrapped a towel round his neck and walked over to the door. En route he paused – and thumped hard at the speed-ball. Then he turned back to Terry. 'I could still punch holes in you, Tel. You know that, don't you?'

Terry said nothing.

'Know why?'

Terry still made no response.

'Because my lads would be holding you down. So you'll be telling Arthur about our little chat, won't you?'

'Yeah.'

'And you'll also tell him that if he doesn't help me – I'll kill him.'

'Kill me? Don't make me laugh.'

'He's serious, Arthur.'

'Bobby Altman? I knew him years ago in the East End. He used to thieve off thieves.'

'That ain't all that easy.'

Arthur was silent as he considered the logic of Terry's comment. 'How's he gonna kill me then?'

'He'd have a number of different ways,' said Terry quietly. 'He'd have ways other people hadn't even heard of.' He watched the first dawnings of fear in Arthur's eyes with a grim despair – for he knew what he was going to be asked to do.

'You'd better stick close, Terry.'

Then Arthur saw a vacant meter and just beat another driver to the space, after a cacophony of horn-blowing and some shouted exchanges.

'Where's this?'

'Lady Ingram's – where else?'

'Arthur, do you know how deep you're getting yourself?'

'I want our wages, Terry.'

'At what risk? You want to die – well, I won't say – young?'

'With you around, Terry, I feel safe.'

'I don't, Arthur.'

'You're the minder.'

'I'm not infallible.'

'No – I am.' Arthur rang the bell of a period house a few yards down the street. A dog barked and a few seconds later the door was opened by an attractive woman in her thirties, who looked as if she had just stepped out of a page from *Vogue*. In one hand she gripped the collar of a large Afghan hound.

'Lady Ingram?' said Arthur, looking surprised, as well as impressed.

'Yes?'

'The name's Arthur Daley.'

The dog yelped and Arthur took a quick step back.

'Don't mind Beluga.'

'My favourite caviar,' said Arthur. 'And this is my associate, Mr Terry McCann.'

'Beluga!' she admonished as the Afghan yelped again. 'You'd better come in, Mr Daley.'

Once inside Lady Ingram's drawing room, the Afghan continued to sniff suspiciously round Arthur and Terry's ankles.

'Beluga, sit!' said Lady Ingram, and Beluga slowly sat. Then Lady Ingram went to an elegant desk, opened a drawer and took out an envelope. She handed it to Arthur, who began to open it.

'It's all there,' she said authoritatively.

Arthur looked flushed. It was the first time Terry had ever seen him in this position and he gazed at him in fascination.

'Yeah,' said Arthur. 'Course it is.' He slid the envelope awkwardly into his pocket and then paused. There followed a long silence.

'That'll be all.' said Lady Ingram finally.

'Er – yes,' said Arthur. 'Come on, Terence. We'd better be getting along. I have that appointment at the Savoy.'

Lady Ingram opened the door with a bland smile. 'I'll see you out,' she said.

'No matter,' said Arthur. 'We can attend to that ourselves.'

'I'd *prefer* to see you out.'

Blimey, thought Terry, she reckons we're gonna lift something.

'How kind,' murmured Arthur. 'Most seemly.'

As they walked through the hall, Lady Ingram said, 'It is Terry, isn't it?'

'Yeah,' he replied, whilst Arthur frowned.

'I'd like to thank you.'

'What for – madam?'

'For what you did for Billy.'

'I didn't realise you – you were friends. Did you speak to him?'

'He called me from the hotel. He was most grateful.'

'That's nice to know,' said Terry, thinking of Altman and

71

losing all respect for her. 'By the way – how's your old man?'

'Terry –' hissed Arthur, but Lady Ingram replied without flinching or changing the expression on her calm aristocratic face.

'He's very ill. He may even die.'

She turned away from them once she had opened the door and walked back towards the drawing room, calling the dog to her side.

'Blimey,' said Arthur once Terry had closed the door and they were standing in the street. 'That was a bit strong, wasn't it?'

'Was it?'

'You've got no respect for the aristocracy, Terence.'

'Look Arthur – her old man might die – Billy's dead already – and you and me are in the shit.'

'I'm not worried about Bobby Altman,' said Arthur in a pale attempt at bravado.

'You should be.'

'Yeah?'

'Right now, you should be.'

'Why?'

'Because his Rolls's just coming down the street.'

'Oh my Gawd!'

Arthur raced for a doorway and took refuge in it. Terry joined him.

'Who's in the car?' asked Arthur, breathing fast.

'Altman and one of his heavies.'

'They seen us?'

'No.'

'Sure?'

'Stop panicking, Arthur. I thought you had him sussed?'

'Just checking.'

'Blimey.'

'What's up?' Arthur's voice rose to a falsetto.

'They've parked outside Lady Ingram's.'

'Yeah?'

'And they're going in.'

'What do we do now?' Arthur was huddled in the doorway as if he was trying to disappear.

'You'd better make yourself scarce.'

'They gone in?'

'Just.'

'What about you?'

'I think I'll hang around, and see how many other people have been invited to the party.'

'Be careful.'

'Yes, Arthur.'

Arthur emerged from the doorway and, glancing repeatedly over his shoulder, hurried off to his Jag. He drove hard into the traffic, causing other cars to brake, leaving Terry crossing the street until he was walking past Lady Ingram's house at a fairly brisk trot. As he passed, he was able to see into the ground floor windows and he could make out Altman pacing up and down, talking animatedly to Lady Ingram.

When Terry reached the end of the road he crossed it, bought an evening paper and stood on the street corner, reading it. After a while, he saw Altman leaving the house with one of his henchmen. They got into the Rolls and Terry could see that Altman was still talking excitedly, but it was impossible to make out the expression on his face. Then the Rolls drove away.

Having made sure that the coast was clear, Terry strolled back to Lady Ingram's house from the other side of the street, only to discover the lady herself leaving the house with Beluga on a lead.

'Walk your dog, lady?' asked Terry with a threat in his voice.

Lady Ingram quickened her pace. 'What do you want?'

'It's owning up time.'

'I've nothing to say to you.'

'Maybe not – but I've got a few things to say to you.'

'Leave me alone.'

'I told you – I've got things to say.'

'If you don't go – I'll call the police.'

'Go ahead. But think what you're gonna tell 'em.'

'I shall tell them you are pestering me – threatening me.'

'You can also tell 'em all about pretty Billy – and Bobby

Altman – and how you just paid off Arthur and me.'

The Afghan began to growl as Terry spoke and Lady Ingram stopped to control it. Then she looked up at Terry. 'What do you want?'

'I'd like a drink,' he said.

They went to an exotic bar in Mayfair where Lady Ingram ordered two drinks that contained more fruit than alcohol. In the centre of the floor was a pool in which turtles and an alligator splashed benignly. Despite their presence, Beluga sat obediently at Lady Ingram's feet as the waitress brought the drinks.

Terry frowned down at the fruit. 'Shouldn't this have custard on?' he asked.

'I thought you might be more sophisticated than that,' she said, sipping hers. She seemed a shade more relaxed now.

'I was just trying to think of a sophisticated way of saying something else. But I can't – so I'll have to ask you straight.'

'Go ahead.'

'You're Billy's mistress, aren't you?'

'That's a very old-fashioned word.'

'I must have read it in a book. Let me put it another way – were you and Billy having it off on the side?'

She lit a cigarette with a faint smile.

'Well –'

'And then Billy falls madly in love with you and wants to take you away from all the squalor you live in to the squalor he lives in. How am I doing?'

'Fair,' she replied, drawing on her cigarette.

'But being a villain at heart, he can't think of a nice way to do it – so he has a go at your old man.'

'Not quite right.'

'Why?'

'My husband tried to murder Billy.'

Terry stared at her, the statement taking a while to sink in.

'What Billy did was in self-defence,' she continued.

'You told the law that?'

'Would it help?' she asked off-handedly.

74

'Help me and Arthur, for a start.'

'But would they believe it? I mean – whom would you believe, Terry? A hereditary peer of the realm – or a –'

'Handsome little gangster from Canning Town?'

'You could put it that way.'

'Fancy another fruit salad?'

'I wouldn't mind.'

Terry signalled to the waitress and then continued his inquisition. 'So, while the two of them were fighting for your affections – what the hell were you doing?'

'Nothing much,' she replied blandly.

'What was the plan, then? Were you gonna run away with Billy?'

'I don't know. Maybe.' She stubbed out her cigarette.

'Was that why he nicked the money?'

'What money?' she muttered.

Terry spoke bitterly, 'Come on, duchess – don't give me all that for Christ's sake. Bobby Altman lost seventy grand. Billy had it – and Billy hid it. My guess is that pretty Billy thought that would be enough to keep you in the style to which you are accustomed.' Terry ended on a mocking note and it produced anger in Lady Ingram for the first time.

'What the hell does it matter to you anyway?' she asked viciously.

'Not a lot,' replied Terry with irony. 'It's just that Altman thinks Arthur's keeping the money and if he don't get it back he's gonna kill Arthur. And as I'm supposed to look after Arthur maybe he'll have a pop at me an' all.'

'I thought that's what you were paid for.'

Terry stared at Lady Ingram for a minute and then said, 'I wonder what Billy saw in you? Couldn't have been your heart of gold, could it?'

Lady Ingram rose to her feet. She seemed quite unruffled and her beautiful face was expressionless. 'I must go now.'

'Not so fast, duchess.' Terry grabbed her wrist.

'You're hurting me,' she said.

'Oh dear – but I won't delay you long. As everyone's so heavily into friendship and doing favours – I wonder if you would do me one?'

'Such as?'

'Get your old man to tell the law the truth.' He let her wrist go and without saying another word, Lady Ingram led the Afghan past him. For a moment the dog looked back at him.

Then she said, 'You'd better come with me.'

Terry sat alone in the reception area of Charing Cross Hospital. After some time, Lady Ingram emerged from a corridor. She crossed the floor and spoke quietly to Terry, 'They won't let anybody else see him.'

'You tell him about me?'

But before she could answer, Terry felt a sickening sensation in the pit of his stomach as a familiar face hove into view.

'What the hell are you doing here?' asked Inspector Barrett.

'Friend of the family,' replied Terry.

'Mr McCann wanted to see my husband,' explained Lady Ingram.

'Did he? How considerate.' Inspector Barrett beamed at Terry, as if giving him the aura of a minor saint. 'I believe he's making a bit of a recovery,' he said to Lady Ingram.

'He's much better, thank you.'

'That's good – in fact we've got good news all round.'

Terry looked up at Barrett but he had his attention focused on Lady Ingram.

'They just fished Billy Gilpin's body out of the sea.'

Once again Lady Ingram was expressionless as Terry's gaze flashed up at her. 'Has anyone identified the body?' she asked.

Barrett, looking as if he was really enjoying himself, said, 'Oh yes – his sister's just been down there. Tide had carried him well out. Feller thought he'd hooked a nice piece of Dover sole – and up comes Billy boy. I was just going to let Lord Ingram know, milady.'

'Thank you.'

Barrett looked at her very closely for a moment – and then walked slowly away.

Suddenly he paused, and looked back at Terry.

'If you will pardon the expression, Terry, this might let you off the hook.'

He walked on towards the corridor and disappeared. When he had gone, Terry took hold of Lady Ingram's arm. At once he could sense that she was rigid with shock. But to all outward appearances, she still seemed very self-composed.

'Do you believe him?' she asked.

'Why not?'

'Because Billy was such a good swimmer.'

Terry, still holding her arm, led her towards the exit.

'He was gonna fake a suicide, was he?'

She nodded and Terry's voice grew harder.

'So, all that stuff he told me about depression and tablets and topping himself – it was all a load of crap, wasn't it?'

'Yes,' she said dully.

'And that was all to set me up as a party to a big conspiracy, wasn't it?'

'I don't know.' For the first time, Lady Ingram sounded desperate.

'What *do* you know then?'

She hesitated.

'Come *on*.'

'All right then. He was going to swim out to sea for about a mile. Then a friend was going to pick him up with a motor launch and they were going to head for the Normandy coast.'

'And then?'

'Another friend was going to drive him to Paris – and then he was going on to the South to stay at a villa.'

'Who owned that?'

'A friend.'

'As I thought,' said Terry explosively.

'What's the matter?'

'Nothing really – it must be just great having all these friends.'

That night, Arthur, carrying a very elaborate executive-style overnight bag, left his flat and headed for his Jag, which was parked in the drive. He got in, revved the engine and had just edged out into the street when he was overtaken by a Granada Ghia which crowded him abruptly into the kerb with a squealing of brakes.

Two of Altman's men got out and advanced on Arthur who was trying to lock the doors of the car from the inside. But he was too late as one of the heavies threw open the front passenger door and peered inside.

'Hallo, Arthur,' he said.

Terry was on the phone in the smoky atmosphere of the Winchester Club.

'Didn't he leave a message for me then? No – it's O.K. I'll have to hang on until he shows up. Cheers.'

He put the phone down and crossed to the bar.

'Couple of G and T's, Dave.'

'No lager, Terry?'

'No lager.'

Dave poured out the drinks and winked at Terry.

'Bit of class you got over there, Terry.'

'Mm?'

'Unusual to see the likes of her in here.'

'She's slumming.'

'Thought that was it.'

Terry took the drinks over to Lady Ingram who was sitting at a table in the furthest and darkest corner of the Winchester Club.

'Slice of lemon O.K.? That's all they had in the way of fruit.'

She smiled. 'It's fine.' She looked around her. 'So this is the natural habitat of Terry McCann, is it?'

'I'm surprised Billy didn't take you to places like this.'

'He was a champagne man.'

'So he kept telling me. This is where he belonged though – I mean – what was he? Just a little thief.'

'You're the same species, are you?'

'I don't steal – and I wouldn't land a pal in trouble. That's how I treat me friends.'

'So you beat people up for a living instead?'

'Who told you that?' asked Terry indignantly. 'All I do is escort a few drunks to the door. Sometimes I look after people who can't look after themselves. I don't cause trouble – I stop it!'

'And how do you recognise trouble, Terry?' she asked innocently.

'It's not that difficult. You soon know when it's just booze that's talking. The fellers who keep telling you how many fights they've had are no threat. Then there are the ones with the bold blue eyes and the smart suits who think they've been in *The Day of the Jackal*.' Terry gave a derisive laugh. 'They're terrific at shouting at birds in the typing pool – but when it comes to the action – they're non-starters. In my game, see, you don't look for trouble: you just keep an eye out for the guys who can cause trouble.'

'So, you're always right, are you, Terry?'

'Not always. There's one lot I can never tell.'

'What are they?'

'Nutters.'

'What do they look like?'

'That's the hard bit – they look like anybody. Even you, duchess.'

'So, I could be trouble, could I?'

'Well – you've caused a fair bit so far.'

'I suppose I have.'

'How come you're involved with a burk like Altman?'

'Money.'

'How can that be? You've got a title – a fancy house.'

'Ever heard of the new poor – the impoverished aristocracy?'

'I keep seeing their houses up for sale in *Country Life*.'

'You buy it?'

'I read it at the dentist.'

Lady Ingram smiled again – but this time much more warmly. She lit a cigarette and as she did so, her hand trembled. Once again, Terry realised the strain she was going through – a strain so well covered by her outward calm. He found himself admiring her courage – and her tenacity.

'So you and your old man were the front for Altman? Poncing round Europe and flogging dodgy bearer bonds?'

'That's about it.'

'Altman must have loved that.'

'Of course he did. New money craves old respectability.'

'So why screw it up by falling for pretty Billy?'

She was quiet for a moment. Then she said, 'He was good company.'

'My mum used to say that about our old Labrador.'

'I would have liked your old Labrador.'

'What are you, duchess?'

'I don't understand –' For a moment she looked vulnerable. Then the blandness returned.

'Are you a villain's groupie?'

'No,' she paused again, 'I loved Billy.'

'Yeah, maybe you did. But he ain't coming back, is he?' The hard note had returned to Terry's voice.

'No,' she said slowly. 'He's not.'

'He doesn't need the money any more.'

'Does Altman?'

'Oh yes – he needs it all right. He needs it a lot more than the old respectability. Altman needs it enough for you to be in a twin bed beside your old man if I tell him about you and Billy.'

'And would you?'

Terry stared back at her impassively.

'Matter of fact I would.'

She started – and he saw the fear in her eyes – just as he had seen the fear in Arthur's.

'For God's sake – why?'

'Because I've got a friend too,' Terry said quietly.

'You look older, Arthur.'

Altman stood in the cellar wearing a dark lounge suit and dabbing at his mouth with a table napkin. Arthur had a cut on his cheek and looked dishevelled. But the main aura that came from him was fear. There was silence in the cellar except for the hum of the central heating boiler and the cracking knuckles of one of the two heavies that had been attending Arthur. Altman frowned at the knuckle-cracking and it stopped.

'Hallo, Bob,' said Arthur in a desperate attempt at

bonhomie. 'Bit of a misunderstanding, eh?'

'I said not to hurt him,' said Altman.

'He got a bit lippy in the motor,' said one of the heavies.

Altman caught sight of Arthur's overnight bag and he unzipped it, scattering pyjamas, shaving gear and a toothbrush. 'Well, isn't that a surprise, Arthur?'

'Eh?'

'I was expecting seventy grand.'

'You got it all wrong, Bob. All I did –'

Suddenly Altman lost his temper. 'Shut up, Arthur. I heard it all from Terry. Did he give you my message?'

'Yes,' replied Arthur hopelessly.

'You thought – a few nights in a hotel and they'll forget about it.'

'No, I –'

'Of course you did, Arthur. Then you heard Billy had been fished out and you thought – bingo – it's Christmas!'

'I haven't heard nothing.'

'Don't lie.' Altman came very close to Arthur and he backed quickly away. 'I can't stand a thief and I can't stand a liar. You don't change, do you? You were nothing in the old days, and you're nothing now.' Altman made a determined effort at self-control. 'See – you got me upset now and I don't like being upset.' He touched the cut on Arthur's cheek. 'I don't like violence and I've got to try and calm down.'

'Sorry about that,' said Arthur pathetically.

'It couldn't have happened at a worse time, Arthur. I'm entertaining a feller from the Department of the Environment, a local planning officer and a merchant banker friend. You're a great inconvenience, Arthur.'

'Bobby – all I did was to –'

'Shut up.' He turned to the heavies. 'Give him a camp bed and a lilo. We'll make an early start, Arthur.'

'Bob. It's all a mistake –' came the faint and plaintive whine from Arthur. But Altman had gone.

Arthur had a terrible night, tossing and turning, wondering what Altman was going to do to him. If only he could be at home with 'er indoors. If only Terry could rescue him. If only

– but nothing happened throughout the long, miserable night and finally, at about seven a.m. he was rudely awakened and taken to Altman's gym.

When Arthur staggered in, unshaven and looking exhausted, Altman was in his track suit and was just tying the lace of his running shoes. Arthur waited patiently until Altman finally acknowledged him.

'Bit warm in the cellar, was it, Arthur?'

'No,' said Arthur obsequiously. 'It was fine.'

'You look a mess.' There was a steely note in Altman's voice. 'Get your clothes off.'

'Eh?'

'I said – undress.'

'What for, Bob?'

'Because I said so.'

'Look,' Arthur's voice took on a pleading note, 'honest to God – you've got it all wrong. Go to my house – turn it upside down – you'll find no money. I mean – you might find a few bob there, but you won't find *your* money,' Arthur gabbled.

'I believe you. You've hidden it somewhere else.'

'On my baby's life I haven't.'

But Altman's patience was wearing thin. 'Clothes off.'

'What are you gonna do?'

Altman laughed. 'You think it's torture, don't you? Electrodes on the private parts – that kind of thing. What do you think we are – some nasty little South London mob?'

'Of course not, Bob. I've always –'

'Shut up, Arthur.'

'Sorry, Bob.'

'We're in happy Hampstead, Arthur. London's lung – that's what someone called it. Fresh air, open space, trees, squirrels, even foxes. That's why I live here – it's so healthy.' He turned to a heavy. 'Don't just stand there, Stuart. Give Arthur his gear.'

Stuart handed a mystified Arthur a track suit and running shoes.

'We're going for a run.'

'Eh?'

'One foot in front of another. Very fast.'

Arthur tried to laugh but it sounded like a sob. 'I don't run.'

'I do five miles every day. Look at me.' Altman patted his flat stomach. 'I want to do the same thing for you, Arthur.'

'No.'

'But I insist. We're about the same age, aren't we? And I'm in perfect condition. They knocked a bit off me insurance premium too. Can you believe that? They actually said, "You're in such good nick, Mister Altman. That makes you a good risk." But look at you, Arthur – flabby, too much of the old vodka. Still smoke cigars, do you?'

Arthur nodded miserably.

'Still chasing the young birds. You could lose two stone – no bother. Change your life – change your whole outlook.'

Stuart took off Arthur's jacket for him.

'Come on, Arthur,' said Altman. 'Shirt – trousers –'

Arthur tried to remove his shoes but lost his balance.

'Sit down and do it, Arthur. Your co-ordination is bad – you're not getting enough oxygen. Know what a run does?' Altman continued as Arthur struggled to undress. 'Clears the mind – business problems float away – and a clear mind helps the memory. Things come back to you – a surprising number of things.'

Arthur was now tugging on his track suit trousers.

'I don't run, Bob.'

'Don't?'

'Can't.'

'You will.'

'I'll die.'

'Now that would be a shame. But maybe your memory'll come back before you croak. Let me tell you, I had a Cartier watch – and one day I couldn't find it anywhere. I even got to the sad point where I thought one of the lads had nicked it – or the au-pair. I even shouted at my dear wife. So I went for a run and what do you think, Arthur?'

'I don't know what to think, Bob.'

'My memory came back.'

'Well –'

'I remembered I'd left my Cartier watch in my tweed jacket. How about that?'

'Very good, Bob.'

'That run found me a couple of grand's worth of watch.'
Altman smiled at Arthur, who was now wearing the track
suit which looked most out of place on him.

'There you are, you look fitter already. And now, Arthur,
I'm going to see what a good run does for your memory.'

Terry saw Arthur's Jag parked with two wheels up on the
pavement and he slowed down his old car in surprise. Arthur
would never leave his beloved vehicle in such a precarious
position. Suddenly the surety came over him – if Arthur
would never have left his car like that, then somebody made
him do it. And there was only one person who could have
done that. Without bothering to get out of his car, Terry
simply changed gear and drove off fast. Arthur was in
trouble, and he was pretty sure where the trouble was.

Altman, Arthur and Stuart crossed the road from Altman's
house to the Heath. Stuart had come along to keep an eye
out, whilst Altman was there to ensure Arthur ran.

'I'll tell you what, Arthur,' said Altman laughing. 'You
could try a runner.'

'Look, Bob,' said Arthur in a last burst of desperation.
'Jogging isn't my game.'

'It soon will be,' replied Altman mercilessly. 'Now Arthur,
on your mark, get set – go.' He set off at an easy loping pace
with Arthur alongside him. Meanwhile, Stuart got into the
car and gently coasted after them.

'Easy, isn't it?' said Altman.

Arthur gave a nervous grin. 'Yeah.'

A few minutes later, however, Arthur began to falter.
Altman slowed down and tugged at Arthur's arm.

'Come on, Arthur.'

'I can't go on.'

'Of course you can.' He grabbed Arthur's arm again and
propelled him into stumbling, struggling action. 'You've got
to understand one thing, Arthur.'

'What's that?' he puffed.

'The toughest bit comes on the second mile.'

'Oh my Gawd.'

'Lots of doctors don't approve of this if you're out of condition. They always say – never try too much, too soon.'

'Do they?'

'You could have a coronary, you see.'

'I've got a pain.'

'Indigestion, Arthur.'

'I'm having a coronary.'

'No.'

'I've got to stop.'

'I wouldn't do that. You might just find Stuart getting out of the car. And he doesn't like getting out of cars.'

'Please, Bob –' gasped Arthur.

'Now, with some fellers – it's their legs that go first,' Altman was jogging effortlessly now, 'like old fighters. Then the chest starts to get tighter.'

Arthur gave a cry of pain.

'You all right, Arthur?'

'It's bleeding McCann,' Stuart said aloud as Terry's old Ford passed the Granada. Stuart put his foot down and began to close in on Terry. He pulled out to overtake but Terry jammed on his brakes and Stuart overshot him, mounting the grass verge that ran beside the Heath. In panic, Stuart realised that the Granada was out of control as it tore over the uneven surface. He saw the steep incline coming and wrestled with the wheel, desperate to avoid it. But he was too late – and the Granada left the ground on the top of the incline and began to fly. Transfixed, Stuart screamed his guts out behind the wheel until the car began to turn over. It eventually crashed onto the track below, upended on its roof and apart from the hissing of the burst radiator, and the agitated calls of the surrounding birdlife, there was silence. Soon the birds settled down – and the radiator stopped hissing. The silence was complete.

'What the hell was that?'

'Let's – stop – find – out –' gasped Arthur as they reacted to the crash, somewhere on the Heath behind them.

'Keep going, Arthur.'

'But –'

'I said – keep going. And step it up a bit.'

Arthur nodded, gulping air, and Altman gave him a push, quickening his own pace as he did so. They entered a small woodland and Arthur stumbled. But Altman simply grabbed him and pushed him on, saying, 'Ever read the statistics?'

'What?' gasped Arthur.

'The amount of old guys who have heart attacks running.'

But Arthur was so out of breath now, that he could not reply. He barely had the strength to nod his head.

'Alarming really.' He began to increase the pace again and Arthur let out a little whine of protest. 'But that's the joy of what we're doing. You see, Arthur, if you drop dead – what do they find? Just another old jogger who's been trying too hard.'

But Arthur was in real difficulty now, gasping and grey in the face. His breath was coming in little short bursts and he staggered with his head down.

'Where's the money, Arthur?' asked Altman.

'Don't know.'

'You can stop, if you tell me.'

'Don't know.'

'Then run!' Altman increased the pace again and gave Arthur's arm another sharp tug. With great effort, Arthur looked up to the sky almost praying for help. He could see the branches of the trees as if through a mist and little red spots danced in front of his eyes.

'The money, Arthur?'

'Don't –'

'Step it up. Come on.' Altman dealt Arthur a vicious blow in the small of the back and somehow he staggered forward, his legs feeling like ton weights.

'Been abusing your body, haven't you, Arthur?'

'You're killing me.'

'The money, Arthur?'

'I don't know.'

Arthur stumbled on for a few more paces and then stopped.

'Please. I can't – go on.'

He was gulping air and his face was ashen.

'Nice, big, deep breaths,' said Altman. 'And then you can tell me.'

'I – dunno – gospel.'

'Oh dear. Naughty stories again.'

Altman began to push Arthur forward. 'One, two, three – and off we go.'

But Arthur's legs seemed to have become jelly and he staggered around like a wounded buffalo. Altman, meanwhile, ran effortlessly backwards, waiting for Arthur to collapse. He was ten yards or so ahead of Arthur when a bulky object dropped at his feet and he nearly fell over it.

'What the hell?' Altman stared unbelievingly down at his feet. Lying on the grass was a Gucci briefcase.

Terry stepped unsmilingly from behind some bushes as Altman darted at the bag, picked it up and unzipped it.

'It's great what a bit of exercise does,' said Altman gleefully. 'It brings pennies from heaven.'

'Stars is what you'll see,' said Terry and he neatly gave Altman a right-hander to the jaw. Slowly Altman went down – and stayed down. Terry then looked across to the glade to Arthur, who was leaning against a tree, eyes staring and fighting for breath.

'Look out, Tel,' Arthur managed to gasp out.

Stuart burst through the trees, a livid bruise above his left eye – and a spanner in his right hand. Stuart launched himself with a cry of hatred at Terry and then suddenly paused in mid-air as Terry's knee caught him in the stomach. He collapsed on the grass and his gasping equalled Arthur's. As Terry turned back to Altman, he saw him stir, pull the bag towards him and open it. He stared down at the money inside.

'You're never gonna count it now, are you?' asked Terry.

'No Terry. You've got an honest face.'

Terry then crossed over to the tree, where Arthur was still leaning, his breathing just a little slower. The sweat poured down over his grey features as Terry said:

'You O.K., Arthur?'

'I'm a goner.'

'Big deep breaths now.'

'I'm dying, Tel.'

'Do what I say, Arthur – just do what I say. Nice and deep.'

Arthur gave a wheezy kind of death rattle and Terry said, 'Now, come on.' He put Arthur's right arm round his shoulders and began to lead him away from the still recumbent Stuart and Altman, who was absorbed in looking at the contents of the briefcase. As they passed, he looked up.

'He'll never make a jogger,' said Altman.

'No,' said Terry.

'You – bastard –' gasped Arthur.

'But he'll always make a runner.'

'Yeah.'

Terry continued to half carry, half drag Arthur along. But soon, Arthur was leaning against a tree. 'Give me a minute – just a minute. But his greyness was lifting and Terry sighed, knowing that Arthur would milk his exhaustion to the last degree. 'I'm going, Terry.'

'Where, Arthur?'

'I'm gone. Honest to God. I need the kiss of life.'

'With your boat-race – you gotta be joking.'

'I'm a goner, Tel. You can have my watch. Take care of 'er indoors. But don't say too much – oh my Gawd.'

'Come on, Arthur.'

Terry put Arthur's arm round his shoulders again and helped him through the bushes to where the old Ford was parked on the road that ran by the Heath.

'Terry,' said Arthur, making a slight recovery.

'Yeah.'

'You know what?'

'No.'

'You're a pal. A real pal.'

'You just can't get by without them, can you?' said Terry.

PART THREE

Arthur took to his bed for a week after his jog and Terry found himself continually attending the invalid, bringing him all kinds of goodies and watched cynically by 'er indoors. But after the eighth day of bringing newspapers and whisky, looking after little deals and having to take freezers, shirts and even a new hoover to various contacts who were being done favours, Terry rebelled.

'We can't go on like this, Arthur.'

'You don't know what I've been through, Terry.'

'You don't know what I'm going through now, Arthur.'

'I was almost a goner.'

'Yeah.'

'It was a miracle I survived.'

'Yeah.'

'So the least you can do, Terry, is to help my recovery.'

'What do you want now, Arthur?'

'Look – if you could slip down to Balham and see Charlie Pierce about those radiators. Then you could nip into Bert Dingwell in Dartford –'

'Dartford!'

'And on the way back I need to see if Smiler Grey has coughed up those video recorders.'

'Where's he?'

'Chingford.'

'Christ!'

'Now, this afternoon, Terry –'

'Yeah?' Terry's voice was utterly weary.

'Nip down to the lock-up and see all's well there. And then –'

Terry stood up. 'I'm off.'

'But I haven't finished.'

'I have.'

'Terry –'

'Look, Arthur, you've given me a day's work. Let me get on with it.'

'When will you be back?' asked Arthur plaintively.

'With this lot – 'bout midnight I would reckon.'

'You can't leave me alone that long.'

'There's 'er downstairs.'

'She won't even bring me up a cup of tea.'

'I'll ask her.'

'No, don't do that.' Arthur looked terrified. 'She's in a mood. Tell you what, Tel – before you go off on your little jaunts, nip down to the off-licence and get me a bottle of whisky.'

'Oh, Arthur –'

'Now.' There was a testy note in Arthur's voice.

'Where's the money, Arthur?'

'Now, Terry, don't be selfish. How could I have got to the bank lying on my bed of suffering?'

'So what do I do?'

'Sub me, Terry. Sub me. After all – what are friends for?'

T.P. Mooney was fifty-eight – clean but not well-dressed. He stood at the corner of a busy junction, waiting for the traffic lights to go red. Then, with a pronounced limp, he hobbled up to a BMW, signalling to the driver as he made his unsteady progress. Reluctantly the driver wound down his window. T.P. Mooney, in a soft, lilting voice, said, 'Excuse me, sir.'

'Yes?' The driver's tone was not encouraging.

'I – I have to get to the hospital but there are no buses. Do you – do you think you could drop me nearby?'

Mooney was already opening the passenger door, but the driver seemed unsympathetic to his plea.

'I'm not going that way.'

'Anywhere near – that's O.K.'

'I'm sorry. I'm busy.'

'A soldier of the Queen –'

But the driver's patience was running out and as the lights changed he said, 'Get a bloody bus,' and firmly closed the passenger door. Then he drove off.

'Same to you, friend.' Mooney's soft Irish accent prevented the coldness in his heart coming into his voice. The lights changed again and, this time, Mooney walked across to Arthur's Jag which Terry was taking on his errands – without Arthur's permission. But Terry felt that if he was to drive half-way round London, then he'd make sure he drove in comfort, rather than in his own battered Ford.

'Have you got a second, sir?' asked Mooney, tapping on the window.

'I might have.'

'Oh, it's you, Terry.'

'What do you want?'

'I have to get to the hospital and –'

Terry opened the door. 'Jump in.'

Thankfully, Mooney did as he was bid. The lights changed again and as Terry drove off, he said, 'Do you really want to go to the hospital?'

Mooney settled back in his seat. 'I'm working for God's sake.'

'Sorry about that.'

'I've had enough.'

'Yeah?'

'Well – I thought I'd had a nibble with the BMW feller.' He looked around him appreciatively. 'This is a nice car.'

'It's Arthur's.'

'Haven't seen him for years. How is the old feller?'

'Bit knackered at the moment.'

'How's that?'

'Been doing a bit of jogging.'

'Arthur!' Mooney looked astounded.

'Against his will, like.'

'That's more like it. And apart from that?'

'Ducking and diving – and dreaming.'

'That's Arthur.'

'So what are you doing? Cadging lifts and putting the bite on 'em?'

'It's a living, Terry. You spin a yarn and while you're spinning it, you know you've got three or four minutes to make them feel guilty that they've got an expensive motor and a man like myself hasn't got a bus-fare. It's a knack – a flair – the hospital always gets them. Mind you – some of them like to hear you've just come out of prison. Strange, isn't it? You get a fiver sometimes, tenner if you're lucky – twenty pence for a cup of coffee if you're not. It's a living.'

Terry said nothing, concentrating on the road and feeling

touched and miserable at Mooney's account of how he was spending his life.

'T.P. Mooney,' said Terry reflectively. 'How the mighty have fallen.'

'It's hard times for us all,' replied Mooney philosophically.

'Yeah – something like that. But I used to tell stories about you, T.P. – great stories. People couldn't believe what you did. Then I heard you were ill.'

'That was a good one,' said Mooney dismissively. 'Now Terry – why don't you stop at the next betting shop? I want you to put on a bet for me.'

'What with?'

'This lot.' Mooney pulled out a crumpled wad of notes and gave him five tenners. 'I'd do it myself but I'm dead tired. It's hard work – in and out of cars all day.'

'I'm sure.'

'Banville Lad in the four o'clock at Catterick.'

'OK, T.P.'

'You know what I want to do, Terry? Retire. I'm always thinking about my old Mam sitting in her wee cottage in Donegal, gazing into a peat fire.'

'I thought she lived in Tufnell Park.'

Mooney gave a disarming smile. 'It's true – she does. But I can't think of her sitting in front of a night storage heater in a council flat, can I? We're all getting older.'

Terry grinned. 'Stuff of dreams, eh?'

'Arthur would understand.'

''Er indoors is a sight different from your old Mum. Still –'

Terry parked outside the betting shop.

'Incidentally – if you see Arthur – don't tell him how we met.'

Terry gave Mooney a compassionate and understanding glance. 'Course I won't,' he said.

'He's forgot the whisky,' Arthur muttered aloud. It was 11.30 a.m. and the hoover was making a great racket downstairs. He lay there for another ten minutes and then, with sudden decision, gingerly raised himself up in the bed. 'I'll just have

94

to fend for myself,' he moaned as the hoover increased in volume.

Ten minutes later, Arthur was sitting in the Winchester, with a vodka and tonic and a good line in self-pity.

'Hear you've had a rough time, Arthur,' said Dave.

'Don't talk about it – it was a nightmare.'

'Are we better now?'

'No – my nerves are shot to pieces.'

'I mean – physically?'

'A slow recovery,' said Arthur.

'Do you want the ploughman's lunch?'

'I could toy with it.'

Dave passed him an enormous plate of bread, cheese and pickles. 'Very agricultural,' he said.

Just then a worried-looking, middle-aged man entered the bar and made for Arthur.

'Anthony,' said Arthur, 'good to see you.'

'Hallo, Arthur,' replied the man in a hang-dog manner.

'Dave – this is my accountant. Give him a ploughman's.'

'This on the slate, Arthur?'

'How do you think a man in my condition could get to a bank?'

'All right – all right. Just this once.'

'What'll you have, Anthony?'

'A campari and soda.'

'Dave, get the man what he wants.'

'Yes, Arthur.'

'I must see you, Arthur,' said Anthony.

'I've been ill.'

'I'm sorry.'

'I still am.'

'But we must talk.'

Arthur gave a long, drawn-out sigh.

'Bloody hell!'

'It's important.'

'All right. Dave, we'll have to leave you.'

'I'm sorry, Arthur.'

Arthur led Anthony to a corner table and said: 'Now what's

all this about? Because I've just got out of bed and I'm in a very delicate state.'

'You haven't paid any tax for five years, Arthur.'

'So?'

'They're after you.'

'*Us*, you mean,' said Arthur.

'What is it about me?' said Anthony spearing a pickled onion. 'All my clients are the same.'

'You mix with the wrong people.'

'Don't I know it! They don't hold with the system and it's getting worse. Incidentally, you haven't paid *my* bill.'

'My health –'

'For a year. Here's my statement.' He handed a piece of paper to Arthur, who pocketed it.

'I'll deal with that as soon as I'm better.'

'When will that be?'

'I'm coming on.'

'Good.'

'Slowly.'

'Ah. Anyway the man from the Inland Revenue wants to know about your expensive motor – amongst other things.'

'I've told you –'

'Yes, but you'd better tell *him*.'

'That's why I pay *you* – to tell *him*.'

'Did I hear the word *pay*?'

Arthur smiled reminiscently.

'That's a laugh, isn't it?'

'What is?'

'Money – it's like a fond memory.'

'It may be to you, Arthur, but –'

'It's like something in the dim and distant past – like Stanley Matthews and long shorts.'

'Where we going?'

'We'll nip in the Winchester for a quick one.'

'Aren't you meant to be running errands for Arthur?'

'They can wait.'

Mooney once again sat beside Terry in the Jag. He was looking down at his betting slip.

'You fancy that one then?' asked Terry.

'And if it's not him,' replied Mooney, 'it's two others.'

'Then why not bet on the other two as well?'

Mooney smiled patiently. Then he began to explain. 'There's no percentage in it. The bookies have got it sewn up. So the smart thing to do is to get other people to bet your three choices – and then take a commission from the winner.' Mooney thought for a moment. 'Is Arthur still game for a lark?'

'What – your kind of lark?' Terry said sardonically.

'See – I can't move around as much as I used to. I need a partner – someone straight, honest, hard-working, loyal – all the old-fashioned values.'

'Blimey, T.P. – you talking about Arthur?'

'Yes indeed. He's a good man, isn't he?'

'He's good as gold,' said Terry.

'Well then –'

'It'll aid his recovery, I'm sure.'

'What are you doing here, Terry?'

'I could ask you the same question, Arthur.'

'When you forgot my medicine –'

'The whisky? Sorry, Arthur.'

'I had to rise from my bed of pain and seek succour elsewhere.'

'I see.'

'And what about my little errands?'

'I'll be about them soon, Arthur.'

'How about now? How can a sick man run a business?'

'Look, Arthur, ask Dave to switch on the telly.'

'And waste more of my time?'

'Look, Arthur –'

Mooney suddenly emerged from the Winchester toilet and Arthur exclaimed, 'Blimey! Am I seeing a ghost?'

'Not quite, Arthur,' he said. 'Got the telly on?'

'Dave!' Terry said. 'Can you switch on?'

'All right – all right. Telly mad, you lot.'

'Look, Terry,' said Arthur, 'I'm a sick man – and a busy one.'

'Knock it off, Arthur.'

'Eh?'

'Just look at the telly. You may see something to your advantage.'

He did – for at the end of the race, Mooney's horse passed the post first. Arthur looked a little stunned, as if he could not credit T.P. Mooney with any kind of success at all.

'You see, Arthur, I've got a system,' Mooney explained.

'Yeah?' Arthur looked at him doubtfully, making up his mind that the win was a fluke.

'But I want a partner.'

'Yeah.'

'Someone honest, incisive, hard-headed, courageous.'

'That can't be Arthur,' said Terry.

'Shut up Terence,' replied Arthur. He turned back to Mooney. 'Do I take it that you are making me a proposition?'

'You could take it that way.'

'I'm sorry – we can't do business.'

'Why not?'

'I don't care how many winners you get – I can't strike up a relationship with you.'

'Get him!' put in Terry, but Arthur ignored the comment.

'You're famous for having more strokes than Oxford and Cambridge,' he said to Mooney.

'Hear me out, Arthur.'

'I'm listening.'

'Listen – we put an ad in *Sporting Life* and get a little office with a good address. We also put in three phones.'

'Why?'

'Just a minute, Arthur. We don't charge fees for the clients. They phone us and we give them a horse. All we ask of them is this – if you back, put ten pounds for us. And if the horse wins – please send a cheque or postal order to us.'

'They'd have to be barmy.'

'Never heard of trust, Arthur? Don't you realise that the entire commercial world is built on trust?'

'No, I hadn't got round to thinking that.' Arthur lit a cigar and Terry said:

'I wouldn't smoke, Arthur – not after you've been so ill.'

'Shut up, Tel. Go on Mooney,' he said grudgingly.

'The system is,' continued Mooney, 'you pay your debts.'

'Oh yeah?' said Arthur, thinking of Anthony and the Income Tax Inspectors.

'You work in a factory and they give you your wages at the end of the week.'

Arthur shuddered – that kind of work was obscene.

'Trust, see?'

'Yeah.'

'You win the pools – they give you the money.'

'National scandal if they didn't.'

'Exactly. Trust again. What about rent?'

'What about it?'

'That's trust, too. Of course, there are a few transgressors, like ourselves.'

'Speak for yourself, Mooney.'

'That's why they have laws.'

'And this little project will break most of them. Right?'

'Wrong, Arthur. We're only selling an advisory service.'

Arthur shook his head and got up. 'A few years ago I might have been interested. But I've been very ill and –'

'I'll even put up the money,' said Mooney quietly.

'What?' gasped Arthur, sitting down abruptly.

'And it's my shout,' said Mooney.

Whilst Mooney ordered the drinks, Arthur turned to Terry. 'Has he got any money?'

'He was very flush earlier this morning, Arthur.'

'I see.'

Mooney turned round to Arthur. 'Dave has got a bottle of Moet? Fancy some?'

'That would be very tasty.' Arthur sat bolt upright, drawing on his unlit cigar. 'So you'll put up the dough?' He sounded as if he were a man talking in a dream.

'Yes,' said Mooney blandly, 'I'll put up the dough.'

'Blimey,' replied Arthur. 'This is a turn-up for the book.'

'The Moet is seventeen pounds a bottle,' pointed out Dave from behind the bar.

'Why not?' said Mooney.

'Blimey,' interjected Arthur again.

'Enjoy your wine.'

'Now let's get this straight –' began Arthur, but Mooney was still talking to Dave.

'Can you cash me a wee cheque?'

'No disrespect, T.P.,' said Dave, 'but –'

'No matter, David,' replied Mooney. He pulled out a crumpled wad of notes and gave three fivers and two pounds to Dave. Arthur followed the transaction incredulously. As Dave opened the fridge, Mooney said, 'A drink for yourself, David?'

'Thanks – don't mind if I do.'

As Dave opened the bottle of Moet, Mooney turned back to Arthur. 'Well – are we in, or out?' he asked.

'Er –'

'Of course, you'll need some expenses.'

'Of course.' To Arthur's dumbfounded amazement, Mooney took from another pocket some clean fifty-pound notes.

'Shall we say three hundred on account?'

Arthur's right hand began to hover over the money.

'Of course, Arthur,' continued Mooney, 'you realise I'm investing in your energy and acumen.'

There was a cynical glance from Terry as Mooney gently topped up Arthur's champagne glass.

'Don't give him too much, T.P.,' said Terry. 'Remember he's a sick man.'

'Of course,' said Mooney. 'If you've been ill, Arthur, I don't know if we can –'

'Ill?' exclaimed Arthur angrily. 'I've never had a day's illness in me life.'

'Then what –'

'I've just been resting from some physical exhaustion.'

'That's all right then,' said Mooney.

'As it happens,' Arthur seemed mesmerised by the money, 'you're a very good judge of character, T.P. Isn't he Tel?'

'Absolutely.'

Arthur took the money reverently and put it into a pocket.

'The fastest hand in the West,' said Terry to Dave.

'To a fruitful partnership,' cried Mooney, clinking champagne glasses with Arthur.

100

'I think we should withdraw,' said Arthur.

'Sorry?'

Arthur looked conspiratorially at Mooney and then winked towards Terry and Dave. 'Walls have ears,' said Arthur.

'So I'm a wall –' murmured Terry.

'We should talk in private.' Arthur touched the notes in his pocket and smiled lovingly at T.P. Mooney. 'Excuse us,' he said, moving to a side table and beckoning Mooney to join him.

'Cheers!' said Dave to Terry.

'It's nice to see Arthur well again, isn't it?'

'Yeah – he reacts to money like other people do to antibiotics,' replied Dave.

Ten minutes later Mooney came back to the bar again. He looked flushed and triumphant. 'Sorry about that, boys, but business is business. Do you think you could call me a cab, Dave?'

But Arthur was there behind him.

'Don't worry about cabs, T.P. Terry'll drive you.' Arthur turned to Terry. 'It *was* my Jag I saw parked outside?'

'As sure as ever was.'

'Just borrowed it, did you?'

'I thought I'd do your errands in comfort, Arthur.'

'What a good idea, Terry. Anyway – you take T.P. wherever he wants to go.'

'That's grand,' said Mooney.

'Shall I put it on the bill?'

Arthur looked shocked. 'What bill? This is a favour to a friend.'

'Be seeing you, Arthur,' said Mooney.

'The beginning,' replied Arthur, 'of a beautiful partnership.'

Terry took Mooney out while Arthur shared the last of the champagne with Dave.

'I trust you'll have a successful commercial undertaking with T.P., Arthur.'

'It's a privilege to work with him.'

'Aren't we the lucky ones?'

Arthur turned abruptly to see Detective Sergeant

101

Chisholm standing behind them.

'You don't half creep up on a chap,' said Arthur uneasily.

'That's my job.'

'To creep?'

'You will have your little joke, Arthur. What have we here?' he said, looking at the champagne. 'Rebate from the rates?'

'You'll have the usual half of bitter, will you, Mr Chisholm?' asked Arthur solicitously.

'Thank you – just in the line of duty. Now, as I came in – I thought I saw young Terry with the remarkable T.P. Mooney?'

'No idea. Is it a crime?' replied Arthur guardedly.

'You never know.'

'What's that meant to mean?'

'Well – T.P.'s been very active recently.'

'He's a busy man.'

'Yes, Arthur,' said Chisholm quietly. 'Busy defrauding people.'

Terry drove Mooney through the London traffic. He noticed that T.P. seemed tired, as if his conversation with Arthur had completely exhausted him.

'You O.K., T.P.?'

'I'm fine.'

'You're not ill?'

'Never.'

'What are all these rumours about your strokes an' all?'

'Strokes?' he laughed. 'I'm as healthy as Arthur.'

'That's all right, then.'

Mooney was silent for a while, then he said, 'He's a good man, Arthur.'

'All you want, is he?'

'All I want.'

'Where we heading, T.P.?'

'The Savoy.'

'Eh?'

'The Savoy.'

'You're joking.'

'Now, why should I be? I need a good night's kip.'

A few minutes later, Terry drove T.P. Mooney into the forecourt of the Savoy Hotel.

'How do you get away with it, T.P?' asked Terry with admiration.

'It's just experience – a little bit of flair.'

'Tell me more.' -

'It's nerve. You *have* to believe in it. It's a bit like insanity.'

'Yeah?'

'You've got to make up your mind who you want to be – Lord of the Realm, an international financier, a well-known theatrical impresario. Then, once you've decided, you've got to *be* that person.'

'I see.' Terry was genuinely impressed.

'You need to be a split personality – a dozen personalities.'

'I'll see you tomorrow, T.P.'

'O.K.'

Mooney slowly got out of the car. He was breathing heavily and once again Terry was tempted to ask him if he was ill. But there was something about Mooney's dignity that forbade the question.

'Cheers,' said Terry. 'Take care.'

Mooney nodded as he walked to the entrance of the Savoy. The doorman saluted him, he nodded and then walked inside. Terry smiled at the charade and swung the car round. What a man, he thought.

Mooney walked straight through the hotel and out into the gardens by the embankment. Breathing heavily, he crossed the road and stood by a bus stop. When the bus came he boarded the platform with considerable difficulty and slumped into a seat. Eventually, the bus arrived in Camden Town and Mooney managed to stagger out. Then, with pathetically halting steps he approached the entrance to a doss-house. Nodding to a couple of down and outs at the door, T.P. Mooney walked inside.

'He's just turned over the London Clinic for thirteen grand.'

'What?' croaked Arthur.

'Yeah,' continued Chisholm. 'Open heart surgery and then two and a half grand for convalescence at the Met in Brighton. He's got style, hasn't he?'

'Liz Taylor had her operation in the London Clinic,' said Dave in a voice of awe.

'No doubt,' replied Chisholm sourly. 'I expect they had Richard Burton, the Sheikh of Araby and Uncle Tom Cobley an' all.'

'Well, you can catch up with him in about ten years' time when he changes the batteries of his pace-maker.'

'They'll get him all right.'

Arthur turned on Chisholm in righteous anger. 'Is that the very best you can do?'

'What do you mean, Arthur?' asked Chisholm icily.

'You pursue a sick man when there are bank robberies every minute – there are terrorists darting around committing outrage – rape is rife in our streets –'

'You haven't been interfered with, have you, Arthur?' Chisholm gave him a wolfish grin.

'Oh, very droll.'

'We like to protect our citizens.'

'You don't realise the value of a man like T.P. Mooney.'

'He knows other people's value all right.'

'He was an 'ero during the war – an educated 'ero.'

'Oh yeah?'

'A gentleman of the old school.'

Chisholm's weary smile tightened. 'Arthur – do you owe Mooney money or something?'

'Of course not,' Arthur gulped, realising he had made a tactical error. 'I hardly even know the man.'

Mooney lay on the hard doss-house bed in a tiny cubicle whose partitioned walls were wafer-thin. He shouldn't have been allowed to lie down so early but he had managed to bribe one of the staff. He felt terrible – and the breathlessness that he had been feeling since his conversation with Arthur, would not go away. Around him, however, was blissful silence but he knew that later the night would be full

104

of men talking in their sleep, wheezing, gasping, belching and raving in the delirium of alcohol. He remembered Terry's words: 'T.P., how are the mighty fallen.' Well – he had fallen all right and he was ill into the bargain. His only chance of rising again was the scheme he had discussed with Arthur. T.P. closed his eyes and fell into a haunted sleep in which Arthur managed to bungle the very last chance T.P. had got. When Mooney awoke he gloomily realised that his dream could very likely become reality.

Arthur looked at the long list of names outside the office door with apprehension. They read:

> MILLIGAN MAIL ORDER INC.
> VICTORY VIDEO
> INTERNATIONAL NOVELTIES LTD
> BLARNEY STONE CO
> SPECTATOR TOURS
> ANGLO-ALBANIAN WINE SHIPPERS
> HARNEY ESTATES
> BANK OF BOMBAY
> STOKE NEWINGTON CREDIT TRUST
> SMITH OF NEW YORK
> DARTMOOR GOLF CLUB
> and many, many more.

Arthur opened the door and walked into a tiny office that was crammed with people. In the middle of what appeared to be total chaos, a small, quiet, nimble man was talking to everybody. He was handing out vast bundles of envelopes, answering questions and picking up the telephone, seemingly at the same time.

'Er,' said Arthur, but the little man was too busy to notice immediately, as he threw four parcels at a giant of a man called Jason, a packet of letters to a man with a video camera at the back of the room and one mysteriously shaped parcel to someone who looked like an ageing landlady.

'I would like a minute,' interposed Arthur.

'Sure.' But he did not look up.

'I need an address.'

'Right with you.'

'Arthur!'

In some embarrassment and annoyance, Arthur saw an old acquaintance bearing down on him.

'What are you doing, Ernie?' asked Arthur reluctantly.

'Oriental carpets.'

'How do you work that?'

'Easy. I get the cheque and then I buy the carpet from a feller. No overheads, see?' He turned to the tiny man. 'Anything for British Medallions?'

'Nothing.'

Ernie turned back to Arthur. 'George Orwell, you know. It being 1984 Medallions . . . Royals, Great Battles . . . O.K. But literary things – forget it. George Orwell . . . we done a ticket there. What are you on, Arthur?'

'Er – consultancy,' Arthur replied cagily.

'You can't go wrong with that.'

'Glad to hear it.'

'We done consultancy.'

'Yeah?'

'You know – villas in Marbella. We had a Spanish waiter on the firm –'

'Now, sir,' said the tiny man, giving Arthur a fraction of his attention.

'This is the company,' said Arthur, giving him a card.

'Mayfair Course Consultants. That's nice – you can walk from here to Mayfair,' said the tiny man. 'Oi.' He looked up at a client who was rummaging through some envelopes stacked on another desk. 'Ask, don't take.'

'Bank of Bombay, sorry,' said the client.

'I'm sorry an' all. There ain't nothing there.' He turned back to Arthur's mounting impatience. 'It's fifty "lid" for a week – a long 'un for three weeks.'

'We're a very old established firm,' said Arthur. 'This could go on for years, not weeks.'

But the tiny man was on the telephone. 'So, all you've got is a letter from the Customs and Excise?' He sounded annoyed. 'Well, it ain't my bloody fault, is it?' He turned back to

Arthur again. 'He hung up. Bloody cheek.' Then his thoughts reverted to the job in hand. 'As I said – that's the rate. If you're still in business in six weeks' time we'll have another think.'

Arthur frowned – and frowned again as he saw a window cleaner gawping through the window. Was there no privacy? Then another client claimed the partial attention Arthur was receiving.

'Anything, Mo?'

'Caledonian Forests?'

'That's us last month.'

'Oh yeah. Sorry.'

'A Forest In Snowdonia Limited is what we do now, Mo.'

'Got it.' The tiny man went to a rack. 'Here we are – you got five.'

'Ta.'

'Be lucky then.'

Arthur cleared his throat loudly and the tiny man turned back to him. 'Are we in business?' he asked.

'We expect the first lot in four days,' said Arthur.

'You'll have your name on the door.'

'You need a bigger door, don't you?' He took out five ten-pound notes. 'By the way, I'll need a receipt.'

'Why?'

'Because we're a bona fide business,' Arthur snapped. 'What on earth would my accountant think?'

'OK,' said the tiny man grudgingly. 'But can you leave your own name and address and telephone number?'

'Why?' Arthur felt it was his turn to ask the questions.

The tiny man shrugged. 'Just so they can get in touch – if there are any queries.'

Arthur realised that he had been caught out and for a few seconds there was a stalemate between them.

'If we don't trust each other,' said Arthur, baring his teeth in a smile, 'where are we?'

'My own sentiments exactly,' said the tiny man. 'Arthur – is that the name?'

'That's me.'

They shook hands in mutual distrust but were interrupted again – this time by Ernie, who was brandishing an envelope.

'Mo – this isn't mine.'

'Whose is it then?'

'I dunno. It says "Do-it-Yourself – Be a Racing Tipster".'

With a grin Ernie turned to Arthur. 'They'll try anything, won't they?'

Arthur gave Ernie a sickly smile as he took his farewell.

When Terry arrived in Arthur's lock-up, he found Mooney sitting behind a table that was littered with forms, books and old copies of The *Sporting Life*.

'I've got the notepaper,' Terry said.

'What's it like?'

'Great.' He dumped it on the desk and gave a sample to Mooney.

'Not bad, eh?' said Mooney. 'West One. Mind you, it's the wrong side of Oxford Street – but who cares?'

'Just look at the directors.'

'Guy Ernest, M.B.E. – that's me. I've used that name before. But who's Lucas Herman?'

'And what about Sir John Franklin?'

'That's a boozer in the East India Dock Road,' replied Mooney. 'I reckon Arthur's done us proud. They love a title in this country – particularly the racing fraternity.'

'Where is – Sir Arthur?'

'Looking for telephones.' Mooney picked up a mug of red wine and took a sip. 'What is this?'

'Where did you find it?'

'On the shelf over there.'

'That could be red wine from Warrington. There's no labels, see.'

Mooney took another well considered sip. 'A claret – definitely a claret. A good one, too. I would say Baron Rothschild's Special Reserve.'

'You're kidding,' said Terry.

'Don't forget what I said, Terence. When you don't know – you *have* to believe.'

'Don't tell Arthur then.'

'Why not?'

'He'll certainly believe.'

'Yes,' said Mooney, 'that's why I like him.'

'Because he's a fantasy merchant?' said Terry.

'Something like that,' replied Mooney, taking another appreciative sip of the wine.

Arthur slammed on the brakes of the Jag just outside the underground station and stared, goggle-eyed, out of the window. He had been driving around for some time but now Arthur saw what seemed to him to be a near miracle. Beside the station, standing in an orderly line, were three telephone kiosks.

Bounding out of the Jag, Arthur approached the first telephone kiosk. He opened the door, sniffing at the smell of stale urine. He picked up the receiver, wrinkling his nose as he did so. He heard the dialling tone and looked in distaste at the graffiti all over the inside of the box. There were other signs of disrespect for one of the directories had been torn into small pieces (a strong man?), and part of the dialling code notice glass was broken and scattered over the floor of the box.

With a grin of satisfaction, Arthur went into the second box and experienced much the same situation. Just as he was about to pick up the receiver a middle-aged man, wearing a British Rail uniform, tapped on the box.

'Yes?'

'Excuse me, sir. I couldn't help seeing you trying the first box. Is it out of order?'

'No.'

Arthur heard the dialling tone and put the second receiver down.

'Is it broken?'

'No.'

Arthur left the second box and entered the third, watched by the mystified official.

'O.K?' he asked as Arthur emerged.

'Fine.'

'I like to keep them in good order.'

'As you should, my friend,' said Arthur pompously. 'You the Guv'nor round here?'

'I'm stationmaster.'

'You're a credit to British Rail.'

'Thank you.'

Arthur retired briskly to the first box.

'Er –' The stationmaster still looked mystified.

'What's up?'

'I hope you don't mind me asking, sir, but are you from the G.P.O.?'

'Not exactly,' said Arthur.

'Then –'

'But I am a kind of telephone expert. Know what I mean?'

'Er – yes. Yes, of course.' He looked impressed, but puzzled.

Arthur went into the box, picked up the phone, searched in his pockets and opened the door again.

'I say.'

'Yes, sir?'

'You haven't got a spare 10p on you?'

'Yes, yes of course. Here you are, sir.'

'Thank you. You're most kind.'

'It's a pleasure.'

He handed the 10p coin to Arthur who then tightly closed the door. He dialled the number of his lock-up – and Terry's voice answered.

'Daley Enterprises.'

Arthur waited for the coin to clink and then said:

'T.P. there?'

'I'll bring him on.'

'Ta.'

'Hallo – T.P. Mooney.' The soft burr of the Irish accent sounded comforting in Arthur's ears.

'I've got some good news for you.'

'Yes?'

'I've found a fabulous place.'

'An office.'

'An office with three phones. Good innit?'

'Excellent work, Arthur.'

'I'll be in touch soon.'

'Good – and Arthur –'

'Yeah?'

'I knew you were my man.'

Arthur rang off with a glow of pleasure. Emerging from the box, he found the curious stationmaster still on the forecourt. Arthur looked round him appreciatively.

'Lovely little station.'

'It's almost like being in the country here, sir.'

'Yeah.' Arthur turned to look at a particularly offensive slogan that was daubed on the wall. 'Not much traffic though.'

'You'd be surprised, sir.' The stationmaster looked down at his hunter watch. 'Three ten to Broad Street is due in five and a half minutes.'

'That's nice.'

'We're not dead, you know, sir.'

'Of course not. I only meant – it's not exactly Waterloo. I used to work there.'

'Yeah?'

'It's a rat race, isn't it, sir?' He smiled bitterly. 'Still, it suits me here.'

'Plenty of bunce?'

'I'm sorry, sir?'

'Fringe benefits?'

'Well –'

'Apart from having an excursion to Broad Street?'

'We've got a nice darts league.'

'So you're a bit of a sportsman?'

'I used to be.'

'I was thinking of tips, the occasional drink.' Arthur paused. 'A score in your fist every now and then. Every week?'

'For what?' He was instantly suspicious.

'Untaxed?'

'Yes sir, but –'

'As you probably realise, I'm an area manager for a large multi-national concern.'

'Really?'

'Yeah – I'm dashing around all over the place and some of my sales staff can't get hold of me sometimes. So, I suddenly thought when I passed your station – hey – three public telephones. Then I discover they're all in working order – thanks to you.'

'But –'

'I thought to myself, that's how the staff can reach me. It's all down to productivity, you see. Exports, helping the country – you know.'

'But what can I do, sir?'

Arthur squeezed the stationmaster's shoulder confidentially. 'Now if you could put a sticker on the kiosks, saying Out of Order, between – say – eleven a.m. and two p.m. and keep an eye out for vandals – you'll help the country, me and yourself.'

'But, I'm not absolutely sure I can –'

Arthur gave the stationmaster one of his special, innocent looks. 'I do hope that – I mean – you're not thinking it's illegal, are you? Would I suggest that?'

'I don't know,' said the stationmaster doubtfully.

'Of course you don't,' said Arthur reassuringly. 'But obviously I talked to our legal department.'

'You did?'

'No sweat.'

'No problem?'

'None.'

'I see.'

'Now, apart from that – my proposition is a sight more interesting than watching Jimmy Saville smiling from the train window when he passes through.'

'But, why do you need three phones?' persisted the bewildered stationmaster.

Arthur smiled patiently, immediately picking a vision which he almost believed in himself. 'New York –' he said, extravagantly pointing towards Kilburn. 'Chicago –'

'Eh?'

'Paris, Amsterdam, Hong Kong, Melbourne – there are guys trying to get hold of me internationally.'

'Are there?' The stationmaster was beginning to sound impressed again.

'There's a huge contract at stake – and a lot of jobs for British workers.'

'I see.'

'And what am I doing, you may ask? I'm on the rag and bone to San Francisco and a geezer from Milan gets the engaged tone. That's another ten thousand on the dole, see?'

'Yes. I understand,' said the stationmaster eagerly.

'But if he's got another number, we're in business. Now I'm driving from Southampton to my office in Mayfair and I stop here. Right here. This is the perfect plan – a key point, you might say. But I call it providence.'

The stationmaster was very clearly impressed. A train began to slowly roll into the station and he said:

'Do you mind if we continue this discussion on the platform, sir?'

'Not at all. You have your work – I have mine.'

Once on the platform, two passengers alighted and the train grudgingly departed.

'You see – apart from that – you've got twenty notes of folding green in the bin.'

'I understand.'

'Are you on?'

'Well – it seems very harmless, sir.'

'Harmless? This is vital work for the country.' Arthur's tone was imperial.

'And this is a most generous payment.'

'I'm a business man.'

'Yes, sir.'

'Able to strike an inventive deal that will save the country millions.'

'And help put our boys to work.'

'All part of the service.'

'Just an out of order sign?'

'A simple thing.'

'And an eye out for vandals.'

'I must have these phones working.'

113

'I'll see they are.'

'Good for you.' Arthur wrung his hand vigorously. 'You're a small cog in the export drive.'

'Thank you, sir.'

Arthur swept out of the station, totally encased in his own fantasy. The stationmaster stared after him, bemused and delighted.

Arthur and T.P. Mooney watched the pages spill out of the xerox machine in great anticipation. The print shop was dirty, noisy and cramped and Arthur had already noticed ink on the cuff of his white shirt. However, he was prepared to make a sacrifice for the cause.

'Caxton,' said Arthur to the printer who was studying the page, 'you do realise that's confidential, don't you?'

The printer ignored Arthur's comment. 'It's got to be a wind-up, innit?' He read out. ' "We are selling information. If you phone us on one of these telephone numbers we will give you our considered, expert opinion of three races." ' He looked at Arthur incredulously. 'I just don't believe it.' He stared at the page again, 'It gets better – listen to this –'

'We know what's in it,' protested Arthur.

But the printer continued to read: ' "When you put down your heavy wager, include a ten pound bet for us. That's our commission. You pay only when you win. We are trusting you – just as you are trusting us." '

'A most spirited rendition,' said Arthur icily. 'You should get down to the Old Vic.'

'Old Bailey – more likely,' said the printer darkly.

Arthur grabbed the page from his hand.

'Don't printers have an oath, like doctors?' he asked indignantly. 'And don't answer that. You are a privy to secret information.'

Mooney interposed soothingly: 'Don't upset yourself, Arthur – it's bad for you.' He turned to the printer. 'Are you a betting man, sir?'

'I like a punt.'

'Well – in that case – you, of all people, should know that there is good information, good connections, good sources –

114

that's the only way professionals earn a living.'

Mooney was so calm and persuasive that the printer suddenly began to take him seriously.

'Five thousand people,' continued Mooney, 'wrote to *us*, mister. We didn't ask them to write. Now, shall I give you a tip for tomorrow?'

'What is it?'

'Dunlop's horse in the three-thirty. John is an old friend of mine.'

'Is he?'

The printed picked up a newspaper.

'Yeah – Pancho Punch – third favourite – eleven to two, they reckon.'

'Now, obviously I can't guarantee that horse will win.'

'I bet you can't.'

'But, will you do this? Give me a tenner for the information – or will you give me fifty pounds, less tax, after it wins?'

'It's a good 'un,' said the printer, pretending to be considering the situation.

Arthur said a little too quickly: 'You're talking to T.P. – not the Scout or Captain Cola, or whatever his name is.'

'I'll give you a tenner,' said the printer after some hesitation.

'Take it off the bill,' said Mooney grandly.

'Have you got it?'

Arthur was driving the Jag round the streets near the station.

'I think so.'

'Let's rehearse.'

'I pick up the phone and I ask him for his club number. Then, I say "We've got three horses for you in different races . . . blah, blah." '

'So far so good,' said Arthur.

'Then I remind him to put our tenner on one of 'em – or even the three of 'em.'

'Then what?'

Terry sighed. 'The next guy phones and I give him three other names. Then the next guy gets three other horses and then I get back to the first three when someone else phones. Simple innit?'

Arthur gave a modest smile. 'Most of the great ideas in history were simple.'

'Were they immoral as well?'

The smile left Arthur's face. 'You couldn't even spell that.'

'At least it was Mooney's idea.'

'Well – I wouldn't go as far as that, Tel.'

'Is it or isn't it?'

'T.P. came to me with a half-baked notion. I refined it and turned it into a solid concept.'

'Oh yeah?'

'And there's not the slightest hint of immorality in it.'

'Of course not, Arthur.'

'All the papers give their nap selection, don't they? Well – T.P.'s got the same form book. This is a great opportunity for you, Terence.'

'Why?' said Terry bleakly.

'You're always on about improving yourself. This is an office job, innit? You're a receptionist cum manager. You have responsibility.' Ending on that majestic note, Arthur pulled the Jag to a halt outside the station. The three telephone boxes stood beside it, each with an Out of Order sign on.

'There you are then.' Arthur gave an expansive gesture.

'What?'

'This is it.'

He indicated the kiosks.

'Where's the office?'

Arthur smiled happily at the telephone boxes and a dawning truth seared across Terry's mind.

'You mean – I'm to mind three public telephones?'

'Now, what's wrong with that?' Arthur's voice was soothing.

'Plenty, Arthur. Plenty.'

'You're always saying you like open-air jobs.'

'I'll be nicked,' said Terry hysterically.

'Course you won't.'

'Why not?'

'They're *ours*. Look at the stickers. Out of Order, they say.'

'You're out of order.' Terry's voice became threatening. Arthur hastened to placate him. 'Terry –'

'*No*, Arthur.'

'Terence –'

'I said, *No*.'

'The stationmaster's on the firm.'

'*What?*'

'Look at him.' The stationmaster was hovering on the forecourt and Arthur gave him a cheery smile and a wave. He waved back. 'What a nice man,' he said reflectively. 'Just a simple working-class hero. The salt of the earth.'

'You pick 'em, don't you?'

'You mean, you'll do it?'

Terry gave Arthur a wry grin. In the pit of his stomach he felt a sinking sensation, but he knew once again that Arthur had somehow beaten him.

'We'll see how it goes.'

'Good for you, Tel.'

'Arthur –'

But Arthur ploughed on. 'Nothing would please me more than to accept the inaugural telephone call personally.' He brandished a buff envelope triumphantly.

'Then why don't you?'

'Because, unfortunately, I have to meet with an Inspector of the Inland Revenue.'

Terry gave an explosive laugh and Arthur frowned.

'Nothing funny there, Terry.'

'Sorry, Arthur.'

'You don't have these pressures, Tel. You're a free spirit.'

'Oh yeah?'

'I'm the one who has to fend off busybodies, the marshalled ranks of officialdom, so that you and me can get a crust.'

But Arthur's eloquence was cut off by the sound of the car door slamming. Terry had left him – and was walking woodenly towards the telephone boxes. Arthur wound down the window and said:

'I'll be giving you a bell, Terence.'

Terry nodded his head and said something that Arthur

hoped the stationmaster had not heard.

Terry stared at the telephone boxes with hostility. Then he nodded at the stationmaster, who smiled tentatively but made no effort to introduce himself. Self-consciously, Terry strolled around the kiosks – which did not take very long. Still the stationmaster smiled, as if he was hosting a particularly difficult party. When Terry had been round the kiosks at least six times a large West Indian woman came into view.

'What happen? Everything Out of Order?'

Terry shrugged and there was a pause during which neither of them said anything. It was an uncomfortable pause, which Terry finally broke. 'You want to phone somebody?' he asked.

'Not really.'

'Oh.'

The woman looked at her watch and then glanced at the stationmaster, who decided at that moment to go back inside the station. At that moment the phone began to ring in one of the kiosks and Terry smiled vaguely at the woman, as he opened the door.

'That might be for me,' she said.

'Probably me,' replied Terry.

'Well, my man phones every week. He's night porter at the Kingston Hilton – that's why he got access to the phone.'

'Kingston-on-Thames?'

'Kingston, Jamaica, man.'

'Well – I'll see.' Terry hurried into the kiosk and picked up the phone. He took a deep, embarrassed breath, cursed Arthur silently, and then said: "Mayfair Course Consultants. Can I have your name please? Thank you. Now what we have today are three good horses ... Number One is Jones Boy, two thirty at Kempton. Number Two is Book Token in the three o'clock race at Catterick – and Number Three is Happy Days in the three-thirty at Sandown.' Terry then explained the system and eventually his caller rang off and he emerged a little shakily from the kiosk. But, as he did so, the phone began to ring in the third kiosk and the West Indian woman gave him a strange look. Terry opened the kiosk and went inside, but as he was talking, the phone rang again in the first kiosk and the woman hurried to answer it. A few seconds later she emerged in considerable confusion and went down to the kiosk that Terry was occupying. She tapped hesitantly on the door.

'Yeah?' said Terry, who was still talking.

'He wants the selections,' she replied.

Terry returned to the phone. 'Just a second, pal.' He turned back to the woman. 'Could you do me a favour?'

'Sure.'

He gave her a piece of paper. 'Just give him these names – and get his name as well.'

'Will do.'

She bustled off, whilst Terry returned to the receiver. 'Sorry about that, sir – we're rushed off our feet this morning. Now, where were we? Ah yes – the three o'clock at Kempton and we've got great hopes of this one. Great hopes? No, I'm sorry, sir – that's not the name. What I mean is that we've got great hopes of Flying Duck. Got it?' Terry was beginning to sweat, particularly as he could now hear the phone in the middle kiosk beginning to ring. Putting down the receiver, he dashed into the kiosk.

'Hallo – sorry? Where? Oh – the Kingston Hilton. Hang on.'

Terry dashed out of the middle kiosk and began to knock urgently at the first, with the sweat now pouring down his forehead. An image of Arthur crept into his mind and he mentally put Arthur's head in a noose and kicked away the chair beneath his feet. The fleeting vision made him feel much better. 'It's your old man,' he hissed for she was still on the phone. 'He's only got a couple of minutes.'

She muttered 'O.K.' at him as she gave the name of a horse at Catterick. Terry then tore back to the middle kiosk again and picked up the phone with a shaking hand.

'She's just coming. Sorry? What's going on? It's not easy to explain. Ah – here she comes.'

A few minutes later there was a slight lull. The West Indian woman was still on the phone to her husband in Jamaica, but neither of the other phones was ringing. As

119

Terry lounged against the side of one of the boxes, he spotted four kids across the road who were becoming very interested spectators to the flurried activity around the telephone boxes. They were obviously out of work and their eternal boredom had been temporarily relieved. Just as Terry was studying them – and they were studying Terry, the phone in the first kiosk began to ring again. He sprang into action and with smooth tones, he said: 'MCC – sorry? Oh yes – Mayfair Course Consultants. Can I have your name?' This was becoming automatic, thought Terry, as he grinned at the West Indian woman in the kiosk next door. She grinned back and said to her husband:

'Look – I've got to go now. Why? I have to *work*. Yes work. No – I don't have to tell you everything. I do 'cos you don't tell me. O.K. you be like that. Ring me later.' She put the phone down, heard the phone ringing in the third kiosk, signalled to Terry that she would take it and hurried into the kiosk. Once in there, she picked up the phone, only to the hear the phone ringing in the middle kiosk.

'Can you hang on a minute?' she said. 'We're real busy right now.'

Leaving the phone off the hook and signalling once more to Terry, she ran to the middle kiosk, took the call, came back, took another piece of paper from Terry – and panted her way back to the third kiosk where she had left the phone off the hook. She sounded very brisk and efficient as she said:

'Here we are now. Your name please. Thank you. Now I can really tell you that we have three great winners. Ready? Jones Boy, two thirty at Kempton. Book Token – and I really fancy that one myself – that's the three o'clock at Catterick and Happy Days at Sandown in the three thirty. Sorry – oh yes, about Book Token – well, he ran last month at Windsor and came fourth, but he was coming up like an express train in the last half furlong. You're absolutely right, sweetheart – I seen it on the telly myself.' She put the phone down and turned to see that Terry had been listening to her.

'Am I any good?' she asked.

'Good – you speak like an expert.'

'I always follow the horses.'

'We'll have to come to an arrangement,' said Terry.

The four kids gathered on some waste ground behind the station and developed a battle plan.

'They're a right pair.'

'Couple of monkeys.'

'What are they up to?'

'Dunno.'

'Must be summat good.'

'It's bent.'

'They're making dirty calls.'

'Bet he's a heavy breather.'

'What about her?'

'She gets 'em worked up, like.'

'So what are we gonna do?'

'We could tell 'em they've been rumbled.'

'The bloke – he could turn nasty.'

'Supposin' they're doin' summat else.'

'What could it be?'

They stared at each other in frustrated puzzlement.

'The phones keep ringing.'

'They leg it from box to box.'

'Bits of paper.'

'Our of Order signs on the doors.'

'Funny innit?'

'Yeah.'

'Tell you what?'

'What?'

'Let's muscle in.'

'How?'

'Be heavy.'

'With him?'

'You chicken?'

'No.'

'Then we could try it?'

'And get your neck broken?'

'If we *all* try it.'

They looked at each other again in greater optimism. It was worth a try.

Arthur wore his most angelic expression as he and his accountant sat in the sombre offices of the Inland Revenue. The Inspector, his face set in an expression of sterile disapproval, sat opposite them.

'Employees?' Arthur was saying. 'I don't employ anybody.'

'But you've got a company,' said the Inspector relentlessly.

'Not any more,' said Arthur. 'I mean – I have *got* a company but it's not active.'

'Oh?'

'It's just a sentimental thing.'

The Inspector looked at Arthur incredulously and Anthony, Arthur's accountant, cleared his throat uneasily.

'But when this great country of ours gets on its feet,' continued Arthur, 'I'll be ready.'

'For what?' asked the Inspector, but Arthur did not reply, being well into his stride.

'The sleeping giant will wake and I'll be ready to serve her. At the moment, of course, I'm more or less semi-retired.'

The Inspector picked up a file and began to study it. Then he said: 'But you've got company assets – Jaguar car for instance.'

'That's not mine.'

'But –'

'It belongs to my Uncle Sid.'

'There's no indication of –'

'I said to him – "Sid, why do you need a car like that?" I said. "I mean you being an old age pensioner and all." So I just keep it for him. It's an old man's folly. And do you know what he said?'

'No,' said the Inspector grimly.

'He said, "You use it, Arthur. You not having wheels of your own." Wasn't that nice?'

'Charming sentiment,' muttered Anthony.

The inspector stared unbelievingly at Arthur. 'But you use the Jaguar car for work?'

'Work?'

'Yes – your company.'

'A man of my age? In semi-retirement? No. I use that

motor to take the old people down to the Darby and Joan Club.'

'I see.'

'Or people to hospital – or to poll. I'm into good deeds – charity.'

There was a long pause during which even Arthur looked spell-bound. The Inspector, however, remained disquietingly suspicious.

Arthur cleared his throat. 'By the way,' he asked the Inspector. 'Have you got the time?'

'Quarter past twelve.'

'Thank you.' Arthur glanced at the Inspector's watch. 'What a lovely kettle – I mean watch. I wish I could have – well, just a simple watch. But these days, well it's just an extravagance.'

Anthony gave Arthur a warning glance, knowing that he was now beginning to go over the top.

'Maybe you'll find one in your lock-up,' said the Inspector drily.

'My lock-up?' said Arthur in tones of sudden fury. 'Is that the reason for this interrogation?'

'This is merely an interview.'

'I don't care what you call it.' Arthur turned to Anthony in high dudgeon. 'Didn't you tell the man about my lock-up?'

'I said you had a few odds and ends in there,' he replied feebly.

'Did you explain about my hobbies?'

'What hobbies?' asked Anthony hopelessly.

'I make things, don't I?'

'What things?' asked the Inspector.

'Oh those things.' Anthony was not completely mystified.

'What things?' asked the Inspector.

'Toys, mainly.'

'What?'

'For deprived children.'

'Look, Mr Daley, one of my staff called at your lock-up and saw several video sets.'

'Never.'

'Just a few weeks ago.'

'Now wait a minute,' said Arthur pretending to think deeply, 'I can *just* mark your card on them.'

'Good.'

'They were – er – flood-damaged videos. I tinker with them. Occasionally I get a pittance for repairing 'em.'

'A pittance?'

'Certainly not enough to pay income tax on.'

'Well – how do you get by?'

'The odd crust.'

'Rent, food, clothes?'

'Bingo.'

'Bingo?'

'All down to 'er indoors. She manages well.'

'A little Metro, two children at a private school?'

'I don't know how she does it.' Arthur leant forward confidentially. 'She's an incredible woman. Of course, between you and me, I reckon she's got a few pennies stashed away in the Post Office.'

'Perhaps she has, Mr Daley.'

'Any more questions?'

The Inspector looked suddenly exhausted. 'Not for the moment.'

'I hope I've satisfied you.'

'We'll be in touch.'

Arthur rose and Anthony said:

'Thank you so much.'

'It was a pleasure,' said the Inspector.

Once outside, Arthur took his watch from his pocket and strapped it back on his wrist.

'That was a nice touch, I thought,' he said to Anthony.

'Yes,' Anthony replied doubtfully.

'So I did all right?'

'Well – I'm deeply impressed.'

'I thought you might be. You see –'

'But I'll tell you one thing, Arthur.'

'What's that, old son?'

'They're after you now.'

'What?'

'A tax-man hates a clever dick – and that's what you are, Arthur.'

'What can they do?' asked Arthur truculently.

'Who knows? That's how they got Al Capone on tax and look what happened to him.'

'Charming.'

'It's a fact, Arthur.'

'So they'll be after me. What tactics?'

'Can't tell you.'

'You're the accountant. That's what I pay –'

'Don't talk about payment, Arthur. Not unless you got it.'

'All in good time.'

'They got a thousand different ways.'

Arthur looked suddenly uneasy. Then he clapped a hearty hand on Anthony's shoulder and said:

'You're up to all the dodges, son. I trust you.'

'What's up?'

'How do you mean?'

The kid on the skateboard made a fancy pattern on the station forecourt whilst the speaker swaggered up to him. The West Indian woman was hard at work in one kiosk and Terry was having a temporary rest between calls.

'What's happening?'

'A lady's phoning somebody.'

'We live round here.'

'Nice,' said Terry looking around.

'You don't live round here.'

'So what?'

'We live round here.'

'You said that before.'

The kid was sizing Terry up and down – and he was dismayed to see how relaxed and confident he looked.

'I'm just saying it.'

'Triffic.'

'You gonna be here tomorrow?'

'We use them phones sometimes.'

'You got 10p?'

'What?'

'Then you're all right, aren't you?'

The kid turned away with a sneer and returned to his mate on the skateboard. Meanwhile, the West Indian woman emerged from one of the kiosks.

'The guy on the phone reckons he's gonna put two hundred on Jones Boy. I said to him "Take it easy man. It's only a selection – it doesn't mean it's a certainty." '

'Good on you.'

She looked back at the kiosks regretfully.

'It's gone quiet now.'

'Office shuts at two,' said Terry, looking at his watch.

'Ah.'

'What's your name, love?'

'Petal.'

'I'll tell you what, Petal – I reckon we've earned ourselves a drink. What do you say?'

'Great idea. What's your name?'

'Terry.'

'O.K., Terry – but before we go into the pub I have to run an errand.'

'What's that?'

'I just want to pop in the betting shop.'

'You ought to be out, T.P.'

'Yeah.'

'Why aren't you?'

'I'm not so good.'

The doss-house supervisor stared down at T.P.'s ashen face. 'What's up?'

'I'm sick.'

'You're breathing bad.'

'Can't catch it.'

'Catch what?'

'My breath.'

'Can I do anything?'

'I'll be O.K. if I can stay here. Want some more dough?'

'No – but if the boss comes –'

'I'll get up.'

Half an hour later, the supervisor heard T.P.'s stentorian

breathing and returned to his bed-side.

'What's up?'

'I'm fine.'

'You're not.'

'Eh?'

'Look at you.'

The supervisor stared down at the now blue-grey features on the pillow and the humped, writhing throat muscles.

'Can't you breathe?'

'Bit of asthma.'

'Rubbish.'

'I'm all right, I tell you. It'll pass.'

'I can't take the responsibility.'

'I often get these attacks.' But even as he spoke, T.P.'s breathing became worse until he could hardly draw breath at all.

'I'll call an ambulance.'

'No.'

'I must.'

'No more perks?'

'Don't be a fool, T.P. You'll die.'

With that he ran for the phone, while T.P. continued to struggle for breath. Minutes later, two ambulance men arrived with a stretcher.

'Come on, old son. You're coming with us.'

'No.'

'Look – you can hardly breathe.'

'I've business to attend to.'

'You won't be dealing with anything unless we take you to hospital.'

'I've told you, I'm staying here.'

But at that moment, T.P. began to choke.

'Come on – get the stretcher under him, Tom.'

Then the choking stopped and with it, T.P.'s breathing.

'Oh my God!'

'He's croaked.'

'Well – *do* something,' yelled the supervisor.

One of the ambulance men proceeded to give T.P. the kiss of life, but nothing happened. The other then began a cardiac

127

massage and after thumping away for a while, T.P.'s breathing miraculously began again.

'Now – you're away with us,' said the ambulance man who had been doing the massage.

T.P. feebly grinned. 'I saw a bunch of angels,' he whispered.

'Oh yeah? Can you slide over?'

'And you know what?'

'Come *on*.'

'They were riding gee-gees.'

'That's it.'

'And they were racing at Catterick.'

'I think you should tell us what kind of operation you've had, Mr – Mr Smith.'

'With a Y and an E – Smythe rather than Smith.'

Mooney was lying in the cardiac unit of a general hospital. His bed was screened off and he was connected up to a cardiograph machine. A doctor was carefully examining Mooney and looking ominously at the livid scar on his chest.

'Well, Mr Smythe, this is obviously a recent operation. We'd like to see the report.'

'This was done by one of the finest surgeons in the country.'

'I can see that,' said the doctor. 'Which hospital was it?'

'It doesn't matter.'

'It would help us.'

'Look, if you're a doctor, you're a doctor. I feel as fit as a flea now.'

'You collapsed.'

'Morning sickness.'

'You couldn't breathe.'

'Asthma.'

A nurse bustled in and whispered to a doctor, 'We haven't got a next of kin, sir.'

Overhearing, Mooney said: 'Well – what's it to you?'

'We do need to know,' she said fussily.

'Is it a crime to die without the whole world knowing about it?'

'It's just normal.'

'Is it?'

'A relative – or a friend?'

'Can I phone somebody?'

But the doctor intervened: 'Look – I want you to lie very quietly. The nurse can phone someone.'

'I want to phone myself.'

'But –'

'It's a simple request –'

'You should rest.'

'For a dying man. I've even got 10p.'

The doctor smiled. 'Mr Smythe. You can phone in a few minutes.'

'I've urgent business to attend to.'

'And you've had a heart attack.'

'That can't stop me – I've had dozens.'

'Which hospital were you in?'

'I told you – it doesn't matter.'

'Come on, Mr Smythe –'

'In fact it's none of your bloody business!'

'Very well.' The doctor signalled the nurse to join him outside Mooney's screened off bed.

'A difficult patient,' he said.

'I can hear you,' yelled Mooney.

Arthur paid a short visit to a betting shop and emerged, well pleased with what he had seen. Mooney's form was good and already the winners were beginning to come up. A regular punter and an old acquaintance of Arthur's came up to him and received a surprisingly friendly welcome.

'And how are you, my old son?'

'Mustn't grumble, Arthur.'

'Picking some winners?'

'Not much luck today.'

'Oh dear.'

'You got a winner?'

'I'm always a winner.'

'You mean – your luck's changed, Arthur?'

Arthur frowned. 'I never really tried till now.'

'Oh yeah?'

'You want your luck to change?'

'What –?'

'Do you or don't you?'

'Couldn't be much worse than it is now.'

'That's bad.'

'That's usual.'

'Look – let me give you some advice.'

'I ain't got no money, Arthur.'

'Trust.'

'Eh?'

'You have to trust, old son. Let me give you this card.'

'What's this?'

'Just ring the number between office hours. My staff will advise you.'

'Blimey.'

'I'll be all right, Terry.'

'Where are you?'

'In intensive care.'

'Blimey!'

'Don't keep saying blimey, Terry.'

'What happened?'

'Had a bit of a relapse.'

'What's that supposed to mean?'

'Nothing much. But don't worry. How's the system going?'

'Triffic.'

Then T.P.'s voice disappeared protesting and a brisk nurse's voice came on instead.

'Who am I speaking to?'

'A colleague.'

'Of Mr Smythe's?'

'Of course.'

'Well, he's very ill, you know.'

'That's bad news.'

'He won't tell us which hospital he's been in before. Can you throw any light on that?'

Terry thought of the London Clinic and how much Mooney had ripped them off for.

'I'm afraid I've no idea.'

'Oh dear. You are –?'

'Mr McCann – business associate.'

'I see.'

'Will – will Mr Smythe recover?'

'He's very poorly.'

'Yes, but –'

'He's going on as well as can be expected.'

'Thank you, nurse. Perhaps I could ring back later?'

'Yes, Mr McCann, and with some information, if you can obtain it.'

'I'll try, nurse.'

Terry put down the telephone in the bar of the Winchester Club and said to Dave: 'Pint of lager.'

'Trouble?'

'Yeah – wait till happy boy hears.'

'Talk of the devil,' said Dave, pouring out Terry's lager.

Arthur came bouncing in, walking straight up to the clearly worried and depressed Terry. Arthur, predictably, did not notice.

'Haven't we had a result, eh?'

'Have we?'

'Come on, Tel. I'll have a large one,' he said to Dave. 'Haven't you seen it?'

'What?'

'Three winners,' said Arthur triumphantly. 'We've done it.'

'Great.'

'What I'm worried about now is – can we expect the right amount from the punters? Will they send their fees in, eh? You see, Tel, you've got to realise there's an awful lot of dishonesty in this world of ours.'

'You don't say, Arthur.'

'Now how many calls did you get? Oh, thanks, Dave,' Arthur accepted his large vodka and slim-line with alacrity. 'On the slate?'

'Arthur, I said –'

'David, you can hear we've done well. You'll get it – and something for yourself.'

'Thanks, Arthur.'

131

'Now – how many calls did you get, Terence?'

''Bout three hundred.' Terry stared down at the drink in his glass.

'Never? That's incredible. Incredible.' Arthur was very impressed.

'Say that a third of 'em put a bet on. Well – the starting prices were good, you know. Book Token at nine to two – that's forty-five pounds for us. But – will they send in the dough, eh? Are they to be trusted? I've got my doubts – but old T.P. reckons they will. He believes in trust more than I do – and I hope he's right.' Arthur drained his glass. 'Set another one up, Dave. You're quiet, Terry.'

'I wondered when you'd get round to mentioning T.P.'

'Thanks, Dave. What do you mean?'

'He's ill.'

'He's always ill.'

'He's in intensive care.'

'What?'

'You heard.'

'Oh my Gawd.' Arthur took a hefty swig. 'Who's gonna pick out the selections?'

Terry glared at him angrily. 'You really are a charmer, aren't you?'

'Why?'

'As far as you're concerned the old guy can snuff it and you're worried about his daily nap.'

'Well, it's important, Terry.'

'Is it?'

'Anyway, it's probably a false alarm.'

'How do you know?'

'Give us another, Dave.'

'I'm not putting this up, Arthur.'

'Terry, pay for it, can you? I've had a bit of a turn.' Arthur began to mop his brow with a silk handkerchief.

'Not you too.'

'Illness always affects me.'

Reluctantly Terry paid for the drink.

'Aspirin, Arthur?' asked Dave.

'I'll be O.K. in a minute.' He took his drink. 'When I've had this – when did you hear about it?'

'Few minutes ago. He phoned.'

'From intensive care? He can't be that bad.'

'He is – the nurse told me.'

'Can he sit up?'

'I dunno. Why?'

'Can he read?'

'How do I know? He might be in an oxygen tent.'

'Making calls?'

'I *told* you – the nurse said he was bad.'

'Do you reckon you could slip him a *Sporting Life*?'

'I don't believe this.'

'Look, Terry,' said Arthur, 'I can be a very sensitive man, you know. I should have known. I should never have trusted Mooney from the off.'

'Can I help you?' asked the nurse. Terry stood at the entrance to the busy ward, clutching a plastic bag and looking rather lost. In one corner he could see a screened-off area.

'Have you got a Mr Mooney?'

'Nobody with that name.'

'Ward H6?'

'Yes.'

'He came in yesterday – smallish, about fifty-five with an Irish accent.'

'Oh, you mean Sir Alfred.'

'Who?'

'Sir Alfred Smythe.'

'That must be him.'

'Well – don't you know?' she asked disapprovingly.

'Of course – Sir Alfred. Occasionally he uses another name – Mooney. I mean – that's his butler – his butler's name.' The nurse stared at him mystified as Terry got in deeper and deeper. 'He uses it when he's incognito.'

'When he's what?'

'He's a bit eccentric, you know.'

'Oh yes.'

'But he's out of intensive care now, is he?'

'Yes, but he's still very poorly.'

'Can I see him?' asked Terry giving her a hopeful smile.

'Visiting hours are two to eight.'

'Special favour?'

'Well – I'll see. There's someone with him now.' She went behind the screen. There was a short delay and then she came out with an attractive and fashionable young woman.

'I take it –'

'I'm his daughter, Fenella.'

'I see.' The nurse bustled off without speaking.

'This is what you want.'

'Eh?'

'Isn't it?' She handed him an envelope.

'What is it?'

'Your daily selections,' said Fenella in an icy voice.

'Thanks,' gulped Terry.

'I trust you won't sell them in the hospital.'

'It's not my idea, you know,' said Terry sharply. 'How is T.P. – I mean, Sir Alfred – your Dad?'

'Ill.'

'Can I see him?'

'No. I don't want you to bother him now.'

'I wasn't going to,' said Terry angrily. 'We just happen to be friends.'

'He's sleeping, anyway.'

Terry gave her a paper bag.

'What's in here – racing mags?'

They would have been in there if Arthur had had anything to do with it, thought Terry.

'Just some fruit. Anything else he needs?'

'No.' Then she relented. 'I'm sorry. I'm exhausted.'

'He's an amazing bloke.'

'Yes, tiring – even when he's ill. Would you like to buy me a cup of coffee?'

'Why not?' said Terry with a smile. The day was turning out better than he expected.

Terry brought two cups of coffee back to the table in the hospital canteen where Fenella was sitting. As Terry put down the cups he said:

'I'm sure this is a great hospital and all that – but your Dad

134

likes a bit of luxury – like the London Clinic.'

'I know all about that – it's pathetic. I suppose you were impressed.'

Terry grinned. 'The Savoy wasn't bad, was it?'

'That's what you think?'

'What do you mean?'

'He even cons himself.' She sounded deeply angry.

'Do you know where he was living?'

'No.'

'A hostel for single men – two pounds a night.'

A look of horror passed across Terry's face.

'The humiliation was beyond him,' she continued. 'Sometimes he actually believes some of his stories. You see – he thinks he's one of nature's aristocrats. All he wants to do is to impress people. People like you – and that awful Arthur Daley.'

'I'm terribly sorry.'

'It's too late.'

'Not yet – and besides I *am* impressed, still.'

'I bet.'

'Arthur thinks T.P.'s the greatest man in the world.'

'Because he can run a tipster service from his sick-bed?'

'You don't go for your Dad.'

'Rubbish!'

'Eh?'

'You think on something. Can't you see I love him? He gave me everything – including four mothers. Don't you know the story of my education? That would be a good story for your cronies.'

'You don't have to tell me all this.'

'I want to.'

'You see – T.P. wanted me to be a success. I went to Benenden, you know.'

'What?'

'Oh yes – with Princess Anne.'

'How long for?'

'Oh, a couple of terms.' She brightened visibly. 'T.P. was flush then.'

'And then?'

'There was a term at Roedean, and one at Millfield. I was the gypsy of girls' boarding schools.'

'Did you know why?'

'Not at the time.' She sighed. 'I wish I'd been told T.P. couldn't pay the bills. Also – I never really knew who I was.'

'Why?'

'T.P. was always changing my name – half the crowned heads of Europe were relatives of mine – supposedly.'

Terry stared across the table at her, fascinated by this extraordinary life-style. 'What happened then?'

'I went to Switzerland – and then had a year in Paris.'

'Good times for T.P.?'

'I don't know. By the time I was eighteen I was highly educated, confident, poised, bilingual – *and* on the most wanted list in four countries.'

'I don't believe it,' said Terry.

'That's up to you.'

He was silent for a moment. 'Just a second –'

'Yes.'

'I *do* believe it.'

Fenella laughed. 'I owe him a lot.'

'Not to mention Roedean an' all.'

'Do you know the most extraordinary thing?'

'What's that?' But already Terry was beginning to realise that he was talking to an extraordinary girl.

'The thing is that sometimes he actually had the money.'

'What – you mean when he took you away from Roedean –?'

'I'm not sure *when* – but I know he had it sometimes.'

'So why did he make you assume all those names?'

'He just wanted to break the rules – that's all.'

'A rebel?'

'Not really. Life's a laugh, that was his view. What's he going to do when he grows up?' Suddenly there were tears in her eyes.

'Will he?'

'You mean – will he live? He's been ill before, and survived.'

'I'm sure he will.'

'What's gonna happen when he comes out of this place?'

'He's a very independent man.' She looked at Terry hard. 'You're not beginning to feel responsible for him, are you?'

Terry nodded.

'Well don't.'

'He's so – he gets himself into such a mess.'

'He won't come to my home – and apart from that my husband doesn't like him.'

'Husband?' said Terry in a funereal voice.

'Yes – and I don't think he trusts him either. You can understand that, can't you? He's not amused by T.P.'s stories.'

'Why not?'

'He's a merchant banker.'

'That figures.'

'So I've no idea what's going to happen to T.P.'

'Let me help.'

'What can you do?'

'I dunno. There must be something – I've got fond of the old boy. And so is Arthur.'

'Him?'

'Let me think.'

'Know what he said last night? If I do snuff it I can con my way into heaven. Then he asked me if I thought St Peter took credit cards.'

Terry laughed.

'Does he owe you any money?' Fenella asked.

'No.'

'Do you owe *him* any money?'

'No.'

'And Arthur?'

'I'm pretty sure he doesn't. But you never know with Arthur.'

'There's one thing you ought to know. It worked out for me – just.'

'So?'

'But it doesn't for other people. All T.P.'s schemes end in tears.'

'I'm used to that, from Arthur.'

'Yes, of course. I'd forgotten. They're both rather similar in a way, aren't they?'

'No,' said Terry, 'they're not.'

'But –'

'T.P. – he's got the makings of a genius.'

'The makings –'

'Yes, maybe just that. And Arthur –'

'What's he got?'

Terry rose quickly to his feet.

'Don't let's go into that just now,' he said.

Terry slept badly that night. He had a mixed, recurring dream that involved him in answering the telephone in hundreds of telephone boxes. He ran from one to the other until he began to crawl – and still the telephones rang. All Arthur could say was: 'It's expansion, Terry, it's expansion. Won't you ever understand ambition?' Then T.P. came up on a stretcher with the cardiac machine still attached to him. Arthur gave him a copy of *Sporting Life* and then ripped off the machine. T.P. died as Arthur stood over him shouting: 'Come on. It's not time to go yet. We've got a deal.'

Terry eventually awoke, sweating with anxiety, and, looking at his watch, saw that he was late for the 'office'. Cursing Arthur, he left the flat without shaving, jumped into the Ford and tore off to the station. When he arrived he found Petal with a friend.

'Hi, Terry,' she said. 'Meet Sylvia.'

She introduced him to another West Indian girl.

'Hallo.'

'She's a first class telephone operator.'

'*And* I was a receptionist as well.'

'Nice,' replied Terry.

'I brought her – just in case we get too busy.' Petal grinned. 'What's the nap selection?'

Terry produced T.P.'s envelope gloomily.

'This could be the last one.'

Petal looked disappointed. 'Why is that, man? It's all good fun.'

'Sure – but the source is drying up.'

'Why's that –?'

'Hang on – here's Arthur.'

'Who is he?'

'The boss.'

Arthur parked his Jaguar behind Terry's beaten up Ford and lit a cigar as he strolled over. He cast a suspicious look at Petal and Sylvia. Terry cut in quickly before Arthur could say anything.

'These are your new employees.'

'Eh?'

'Without Petal – I couldn't have done it.'

'You're not talking about wages, are you?'

'Yeah.'

'Look, Terry –'

'No stamps though.'

'I haven't had a penny yet,' mourned Arthur.

'That's your problem.'

'And I never asked you to sub-contract work.' Arthur turned to Petal with a hopeful smile. 'You understand that, don't you, flower?'

'Petal,' said Terry.

'Of course,' replied Arthur. 'Now –'

'So they need dough.'

'For a few minutes of answering the phone?'

'Four hours, actually,' said Terry.

Arthur turned his most ingratiating smile on Petal. 'How about a tenner? I'm well known as a generous governor.'

'Don't listen to him,' said Terry to Petal, but unfortunately, Arthur's fatal charm was working on her.

'I'd be happy to have –'

'Don't say anything,' said Terry.

'Yes, my dear?' asked Arthur solicitously, baring his teeth at her.

'Well –' All was lost – she had weakened at the worst possible moment and Arthur had triumphed.

'That's all right, Petal. You do understand, don't you?' He slipped a fiver into her hand. 'Put that in your sporran, darling.'

'You're gonna hate yourself for that,' said Terry. He turned back to Arthur. 'And what about Sylvia?'

'She ain't done anything yet,' replied Arthur sweetly. 'Now, Terry, have you seen T.P.?'

'I wondered when you were gonna ask.'

'How is he?'

'Not so good.'

'Is he going to –?'

'We don't know.'

'And the –?'

'This might be the last one, Arthur.'

'Oh my Gawd!' Then Arthur looked round and the words stuck in his throat. He tried to say something but merely made an inarticulate noise of fear and anger.

'Hallo,' said Terry. 'Where did they spring from?'

The kids had returned, but greatly strengthened in numbers. Now there were eight of them – a multi-racial gang – and three had surreptitiously occupied the phone kiosks.

'Get 'em,' yelled Arthur. "It'll be business hours soon.' He took a couple of steps towards the kiosks. 'Er – you lot – can't you read? It says Out of Order.'

'You're out of order an' all,' said one of the kids, opening and shutting the door of the kiosk.

'Cheeky lout. I'll have you.' Arthur practically gibbered with rage. At that moment, the kid on the skateboard brushed past Arthur. 'Oi – you got a licence for that?'

The boy said something very personal that made Arthur even angrier. 'Terry – get 'em out.'

'How?'

'With violence. Kick 'em up the arse!'

'They're in business if they've got 10p.'

'What's this? Betrayal?' Arthur paused dramatically. 'I left you here to mind these telephone kiosks, Terry – and now I'm threatened by Bugsy Malone and his mob.'

'You've been tumbled, Arthur,' replied Terry unsympathetically.

Arthur grimaced and one of the kids said to him: 'We live round 'ere.'

'He said that yesterday as well,' commented Terry.

'Terence!' Arthur's voice rose.

'Watch your blood-pressure, grandad,' jeered the boy on the skateboard.

Then, a younger boy, wearing sunglasses said to Arthur, 'Do you realise these telephone boxes are the only ones in the metropolitan area that haven't been vandalised.' His voice was small and menacing and it had a definite impact on Arthur, who looked uneasy. A real villain of the future, thought Terry, and smooth with it.

'That's right, Shades,' said the skateboard kid, circling round Arthur again. 'I mean – these are like gold-dust in your game.'

'What game?' said Arthur defensively.

'I don't know what game.'

'Look, sonny –' Arthur tried bravado without success.

'But it's got to be a bit iffy,' said Shades. 'I mean – it must be.'

Arthur looked as if he was being threatened by a heavy mobster. Then he saw another kid clambering over his Jag and he started to stutter:

'What – what's he doing?'

'He's an aerial freak, inne?'

'Terry,' Arthur's voice was shrill, '*do* something.'

Terry yelled: 'Oi – come 'ere!' Slowly the boy left Arthur's Jag and came across to him. 'Now, listen.'

'Yeah?'

'You can give plenty of aggravation to me and the girls messing about with the phones, but if you harm that motor, I'm gonna knock your head off.' He smiled. 'Understand?'

'Listen to what the gentleman says, like a good boy,' put in Arthur.

The boy nodded, but while he was doing so – one of the phones rang and one of the kids in the telephone kiosks picked up the receiver. Arthur rushed to the kiosk and opened the door. 'What is it?'

'Sorry,' said the kid as he replaced the phone, 'wrong number.'

'You little –' shrieked Arthur, while Shades nearby satisfied himself by saying, 'There's gonna be a lot of that.'

141

Arthur took stock of the situation, glared at Terry and approached Shades with a cagey smile. 'So you're the head-man, eh?'

'Yeah.'

'What do they call you?'

'They call me Shades.'

'Er – yes – now can I call you Shades?' Arthur draped one arm round his shoulder.

'What do you want?'

'I want a chat.'

'What about?'

'I like a young man with ambition.'

'Eh?'

'You see – what we've got here, Shades, is a rupture of communication.'

The boy tried to move away from Arthur's comradely arm but Arthur tightened his grip.

'You come here, team handed, terrorising law-abiding rate-payers who use the facilities of the GPO – to whit a public rag and boner.'

'So?'

'And you expect ransom, blackmail or even protection money. Is that the situation?'

'Could be.'

'Is it – or isn't it?'

'It is.'

Arthur smiled and steered Shades to the kerb and back. 'You see, son, I don't intend to lecture you about the ambiguous morality of the situation.'

'Don't bother.'

'How much?'

Arthur grinned at Terry and said, like a bad ventriloquist: 'The kid's a mug.' He then smiled blandly at Shades. 'Well?'

'A ton.'

Arthur looked as if he was going to have apoplexy. 'You gone round the twist?'

'I said, a ton.' Shades' voice hardened.

'Haven't you read your *Financial Times*? Don't you know recession is rampant in the Western world. We're all having

142

to scrimp and scrape. But you, Shades, you want a hundred notes of sheer exploitation and wanton greed.'

'Fifty?'

Arthur turned to Terry again with his bad ventriloquist act, little aware that Shades could understand every word. 'I told you the kid's a mug.' He turned to Shades with a bright smile. 'Ten – and I'm being generous.'

'Leave it out.'

'What then?'

'Forty.'

'I said ten.'

'Thirty.'

'You're a fool to yourself.'

'Thirty, I said.'

'Twenty-five.'

'A score – and we touch hands.'

Shades thought hard. He did not consult the other kids and they seemed to be listening to him in awe, content that he should hold sway over the bargaining.

'All right.'

'You'll take a cheque?'

Shades looked affronted. 'No way!'

'Just testing,' said Arthur.

Arthur dug into his pocket and brought out twenty crumpled pound notes.

'O.K.?'

'We'll come back if we need more.'

'If you do – I'll see you get your arse kicked.'

'Who by?'

'My man here.'

'Oh, him.'

Shades put his fingers in his mouth and whistled his men out the telephone kiosks. Arthur then took Terry aside, while Petal and Sylvia looked on in amazement at the completion of the negotiations.

'I think he knows who's boss.'

'Yeah – he is.'

'Come on, Tel. Admit I had him.'

'I was deeply impressed,' said Terry ironically. 'Inciden-

143

tally, we haven't discussed my fee yet, Arthur.'

'What fee?'

'Wages? Salary?'

'Oh,' said Arthur airily. 'You'll get your whack. You don't
expect to be a partner, do you?' he asked in terms of amused
amazement.

'Why not? I do most of the work.'

'Terry – my dear Terry –'

'Yeah?'

He put a hand on Terry's shoulder. 'See, you don't
understand, Terence.'

'Understand what, Arthur?'

'The difference between senior management and the
worker on the shop floor.'

'Oh?'

'It's all down to differentials.'

'Eh?'

'Have you heard that expression, Tel?'

'Yes, Arthur. I seem to recall I have.'

'It means – well, the difference between the soldier on the
field, and the General on the staff.'

'No need to say which one I am.'

'Command decisions, you see. Do you understand it now?'
Arthur looked at his watch. 'Oh, I've got to fly.'

'You haven't said anything about money, Arthur.' The old
feeling was coming over Terry – the feeling of resigned
helplessness. But Arthur was half-way across the street,
heading for his Jag. He stopped to point an accusing finger.
'You know what your problem is, Terry?'

'No?'

'It's just like young Shades.'

'What's that, Arthur?'

'Greed – wanton greed.'

'I see.'

'I'll be in touch.'

'Arthur –'

But the telephones in the kiosks began to ring and they set
up such a racket that Terry was reminded forcibly of his

dream. Arthur smiled and waved from the safety of his Jaguar.

'Nothing wrong with work, you know.' He roared off leaving Terry and Petal heading towards the blasting phones.

'He didn't say anything about me working,' said Sylvia.

'No,' said Terry. 'He didn't.'

Slowly Sylvia began to walk towards one of the kiosks.

'It's a miracle, isn't it?' said Terry to Petal as he opened the door.

'What is a miracle?'

'Arthur's rabbit,' he snapped, slamming the door.

Arthur walked briskly down the corridor towards the door with the name-plate on. He felt good, confident and sure that at last, as he had told Terry, he was senior management. When Arthur opened the door of the office, Ernie was standing there with a welcoming grin whilst the tiny man busied himself as usual behind the desk.

'Hallo, Arthur.'

'Good morning.'

'You've had quite a result, haven't you?'

'How do *you* know?' asked Arthur.

'Look at your pile of correspondence – very handsome. Be lucky, Arthur.'

'It's not a question of luck, Ernie. It's business acumen.'

'Oh yes.'

'Experience.'

'Mm.'

'Tenacity.'

'That's it.'

'And above all – courage.'

Ernie shook him by the hand as he left and a volley of imaginary trumpets sounded in Arthur's ears.

'What a clever feller, eh?' cried the tiny man, giving him a cynical smile. But Arthur did not notice and the trumpets resounded again.

'Don't worry about me, old friend.'

'I'm not.'

'I combine honest endeavour with enterprise.'

'Sure.'

'If the price is right there are always customers.'

'You bet.'

'Never mind about supplementary benefits. Get out and graft is my philosophy.'

The tiny man gave him a huge bundle of envelopes and Arthur whistled with appreciation.

'There you are, you see. It's all trust, you know.'

The tiny man leant over his desk and addressed Arthur in a furtive whisper, 'A guy was asking for you.'

Arthur immediately lost his confidence. In a worried tone he said: 'Who?'

'He wouldn't say his name.'

'But –'

'He looked official like.'

'Like what?'

'He wouldn't say his name.'

'So you said.'

'He looked official like.'

'You said that, too.'

'He had a raincoat.'

'And?

'Well – you can spot 'em, can't you? It's the Terylene, innit?'

'What did he want?' Arthur tried not to betray his anxiety, but failed. As he talked he opened a couple of envelopes and a cheque fell out. Arthur looked surprised.

'He didn't say.'

'You must have – did you pick up anything?'

'Right away I thought – it's gotta be Mr Plod.'

'Oh my Gawd!'

'Or even worse.'

'Like what?'

'The dreaded VAT man.'

Arthur blanched and the tiny man continued with relish, 'They knock on the door in the early hours.'

'Oh yeah?'

'You hear terrible things, don't you? About the VAT man.'

'Yeah.'

'Anyway, I thought I'd mark your card.'

Arthur tried to regain his composure. 'I'm most grateful, but everything I'm doing is above board.'

'Of course.'

'All paid up.'

'Why not?'

He stuffed the envelopes into his pockets. 'Must be getting on – probably send one of my staff in next time. Too busy to make these journeys.' Arthur hurried out of the office. 'Cheery-bye.'

'So long.'

Left alone, the tiny man gave vent to a tiny laugh.

'I got him going,' he muttered, well pleased with himself.

'Oi!'

'Yeah?'

Ernie turned to see he was being hailed by an official-looking man in a Terylene raincoat.

'You a friend of Mr Daley?'

'No.'

'You know him?'

'Very slightly.'

'Do you know which is his car?'

'Er –'

'I'm sure you do.' The man smiled threateningly – in an official way.

'Yeah. Course I do.'

'Then –'

'It's over there – the Jag.'

'Thank you. I'm most grateful.'

'It's a pleasure.'

Hurriedly, Ernie departed, knowing he had shopped Arthur.

Arthur stood in the reception area of the office block, scanning the cheques and postal orders that the envelopes had contained. Then he walked out to the street entrance and

147

paused. The man in the Terylene raincoat was prowling round his Jag. Arthur remained frozen in the reception area until the man began to move away. Slowly Arthur stepped into the street, but as he did so, the man suddenly took renewed interest in the car. Frozen again on the pavement, Arthur spied a cruising cab and hailed it.

'Where to, Guv?' asked the cabbie, turning round to see Arthur crouching on the floor. 'You O.K?'

'Just a little warm,' said Arthur desperately.

'Warm?'

'The glass – it reflects the heat.' He doubled up on the floor again, well beneath the window level. 'I'm allergic to light,' he said.

'You planning on getting out?'

'Now?'

'When I drop you?'

Arthur considered the situation. 'If I keep low.'

'Want a blanket or something?'

'No thanks.'

'You're not a celebrity?'

'Well –'

'TV star?'

'Just a successful business man.'

The cabbie again regarded Arthur's crouched position. 'Where to?' he repeated impatiently.

'The Winchester Club.'

The cabbie set up his meter and drove on.

'Right nutter,' he said to himself warily, wondering if Arthur would cause trouble en route.

In the Winchester, Arthur regained confidence on his favourite stool. Dave was the captive audience.

'There I was, more or less surrounded.'

'It was a stake-out, was it?'

'Oh yeah – very carefully planned. Must have been dozens of 'em.'

'But you evaded them?'

'Course.' Arthur gave a modest shrug.

'How did you do it?'

'It was just one of them James Bond things.'

'You wore a frogman's outfit?'

'Eh?'

'He often does.'

Arthur shook his head impatiently.

'None of that – just ordinary raincoats.'

Dave stared at him, puzzled. 'What do you mean, Arthur?'

'What I say – ordinary raincoats.'

'In disguise?'

'I knew right away – one of 'em was a right wally.' Arthur smiled at the recollection. 'You know, Dave, they have to get up early in the day to find Arthur Daley.'

'Arthur –'

'Yeah.'

'Why were they wearing raincoats?'

'They always do.'

'I see.'

'I had 'em sussed.'

But Dave was no longer giving Arthur his undivided attention.

'Hallo, Mr. Sprott. Long time –'

'Hi Dave. How about a bottle of light ale?'

'Coming up.'

Arthur turned, annoyed at his flow being interrupted. Then he almost fell off his stool. Just by his side was standing the man with the Terylene raincoat.

'Now, Arthur,' said Dave, 'I still can't understand this business about the raincoat – Hey Arthur –'

But Arthur was already heading towards the exit. Then Sprott saw him.

'Oi!'

Arthur was still beating a retreat.

'Daley, innit?' But Arthur was gone.

With as much dignity as senior management would allow, Arthur cantered across the street outside the Winchester. But even after his recent jogging experiences, Arthur was unable to elude Sprott who was after him in a few seconds and soon had his hand on his coat collar.

'At your age,' said Sprott, 'you'll do yourself a mischief running like that.'

For a moment Arthur wished he had taken up his recent jogging invitation more readily.

'I beg your pardon?'

'Come on, Daley.'

'Who are you?' blustered Arthur. 'I think you've got the wrong man.'

'I don't think so.'

'You trying to mug me or something?'

Mr Sprott flashed a warrant card and Arthur's indignation quietened.

'Ever seen one of these before?'

'It's not a Fulham season ticket, is it?'

'In the motor.'

'Hang about!'

'I said – *in* the motor, Daley.'

'I don't go with strangers.'

'Why not?'

'Didn't your mum ever tell you that –'

Sprott gave Arthur an evil grin. 'My mum said knee 'em in the privates.'

'Did she? I don't consider that –'

'*Get* in.'

'Well if you're gonna be like that.'

'You going?'

'If I have to.'

'You have to.'

Sprott began to hustle the unwilling Arthur to a saloon car. He opened the front passenger door and unceremoniously dumped Arthur on the seat. He then turned round to the driver's door, shouting as he did so:

'Don't try anything, Daley.'

'I don't understand,' said Arthur.

But directly Sprott climbed behind the wheel it was very clear to Arthur that he was having difficulty in controlling his anger.

'Well?' said Arthur.

'Shut up.' Sprott made no attempt to drive and Arthur

produced his full magisterial tone of outraged injustice.

'I think you should know that I am one of the most respectable businessmen in the borough – indeed throughout the Greater London area and I am not used to –'

'Shut up.'

'I beg your pardon?' But Arthur was beginning to quail.

'You owe me money,' said Sprott in a hoarse whisper.

'Me?'

'You.'

Sprott had a manic expression on his face and suddenly Arthur felt instinctively that he was neither from the Income Tax nor the VAT.

'Could I ask –?'

'Where's T.P.?'

'Is this official business?'

'Answer the question.'

A kind of Dutch courage overtook Arthur. 'I must ask you – is this official business?'

'No.'

'Where we going?'

'You'll find out.'

'To the nick?'

'No.'

'Then –'

'Where is he?' asked Sprott quietly.

'He's ill.'

'You his partner?'

'We have certain common interests.'

'I said – you his partner?'

'In a way.'

'I see.'

'You don't work round here?' asked Arthur, unsuccessfully trying to put the conversation on a less threatening level.

'I don't work anywhere.'

'Retired, are you? Of course, I'm semi–'

'I got kicked out.'

'Redundant?'

Sprott snarled at Arthur. 'T.P. and me were going to work together.'

'Nice,' said Arthur in his most social voice.

151

'I gave him money.'

'Yeah?'

'*My* money. He was going to get an office. I fancied that – a little office with three phones.'

Arthur started.

'Now *you've* got the office.'

'I don't know what you're on about.'

Sprott suddenly grabbed Arthur's jacket.

'You owe me money.'

'How dare you!'

'Don't give me that.'

Arthur was now extremely frightened, despite the fact that they were sitting in Sprott's car in broad daylight. Arthur considered that Sprott had a crazy glint in his eye – and he didn't like it.

'I don't know anything about your arrangements with T.P.'

'It's your office, innit?'

'Well?'

'Come *on*.'

'In a sense.'

'What does that mean?' His grip hardened.

'What I say – in a sense.'

'The office. It's mine.'

'Look –'

'I tell you – I own it.'

'The telephones –' said Arthur feebly.

'All three of 'em.'

'It's an expensive suite.'

'I'll tear it into shreds.'

'Now don't do that –'

'Why the hell not?' Sprott was beginning to look even more manic.

'I'm sure we can come to a reasonable arrangement.' Despite his rising fear, Arthur managed to give Sprott an optimistic smile.

'What do you mean?'

'What I say. I've always been a reasonable –'

'Where is it?'

'The office?'

'Come on –'

'I'll show you,' said Arthur magnanimously. 'All I hope is that the staff are at their posts.' Specially Terry, thought Arthur desperately.

Sprott's anger seemed to increase on the way to the station and Arthur grew even more agitated as Sprott drove erratically and extremely fast. When they were almost there, he snapped out, 'What is it?'

'Eh?'

'Short-term lease?'

'Oh yes. Short lease.'

'What else?'

'What do you mean?'

'Other amenities?' Sprott snarled as he accelerated.

'Oh, it's very handy for transport,' said Arthur evasively.

'What kind of transport?'

'Trains, you know.'

'Yeah?'

'And helpful neighbours.'

The station was looming ahead and Arthur felt a sinking in the pit of his stomach. Sprott wasn't going to like this – and Arthur hoped that Terry would be immediately available. Suppose he was in the pub? Arthur's heartbeat quickened. Sprott wasn't going to like anything.

'Just park by the station,' Arthur said in a squeaky voice.

'Not much of a neighbourhood.'

'Short-lease,' whimpered Arthur, jumping out of his passenger door as Sprott parked. 'Very short-lease.'

Once out of the car, Arthur dashed over to the telephone kiosks. 'Thank Gawd,' he said as he saw Terry inside one of them. Thumping on the door, Arthur yelled, 'Terry!'

But he was talking decisively and concentrating on the phone.

'Terry!'

Still no response and already Sprott was walking purposefully towards the kiosk. His eyes were little hard nuggets of suspicion that was rapidly turning to hatred.

'Terry!'

Again there was no response.

'For Gawd's sake!'

Finally, Terry opened the kiosk door, looking annoyed. 'I'm on the phone.'

'So I see. Look Tel –'

'Listen, Arthur. I'm trying to run a business. Shop floor – you know –'

'I'm being threatened.'

'You're senior management – take some decisions.'

'Terry – I'm being threatened.'

'And I thought it was something new!'

Terry closed the door, leaving Arthur transfixed and Sprott gaining on him. Then Arthur saw Shades and the other kids.

'This is too much,' he said.

'We need some more dough,' said Shades. 'What you gave me weren't enough.'

'Get lost!'

'You want trouble?'

'No.'

Sprott was still gaining, looking around him, with his lips moving soundlessly.

'Where's my dough?' asked Shades.

'All right,' said Arthur. 'I'll talk.'

'We don't want talk – we want money.'

'Just a minute.'

'Now!'

'Can I introduce you to the new landlord?'

'Who?'

'Charming guy.'

Sprott came up unbelievingly to Arthur, his eyes blazing.

'You said this was your office.'

'*You* said it was.'

'On a short lease –'

'Well – you've got certain outgoings, like.'

'Like what?'

'Where's my dough?' asked Shades, and the other kids, knowing that Terry was otherwise engaged, began to crowd in.

154

Then Petal emerged from one of the kiosks.

'Like Petal,' said Arthur.

'It hasn't been so strenuous today,' she smiled.

'Then there's the stationmaster,' confided Arthur to Sprott. 'He's on the firm.'

'This is bloody ridiculous,' said Sprott.

'Then there's toilets on the platform,' continued Arthur.

But Sprott could take no more. He lunged at Arthur, knocking him backwards into a telephone kiosk.

'You're a con man,' he shouted.

'Not at all,' said Arthur panting for breath. 'You don't know the other outgoing.'

'What's that?'

'Terry.'

'Who's Terry?'

'Well he takes care of all the aggravation – physical or otherwise.'

'Oh yeah?'

'I assure you – he's most useful.' Sprott now had Arthur pinned up against the telephone kiosk.

'We'll see, shall we?'

'Terry!' Arthur howled.

'Where's our dough?' asked Shades again.

'Get lost, kid!' yelled Sprott.

'We're in on your game,' replied Shades, not in the least shaken by Sprott's glazed expression.

'You know, Daley,' said Sprott, getting his twitching face very close to Arthur's, 'you owe me.'

'Please desist,' spluttered Arthur. 'I'm a prominent local businessman.'

'You'll be a prominent local stiff,' snarled Sprott.

'Terry!'

'Yes, Arthur?' Terry kicked open the door of the telephone kiosk. 'Did you call me, sir?'

'I think so,' said Arthur, breathing heavily.

Sprott looked up at Terry and the manic glint in his eyes became subdued. 'Who the hell are you?'

'I'm minding the office,' said Terry.

'What office?'

'It's a nice little business.'

Sprott stared hypnotically at Terry. 'What the hell do you mean?'

The telephones began to ring simultaneously in all three kiosks.

'And it's all yours.'

'Answer those damned phones,' said Sprott.

'Why?' asked Terry. 'They're probably for you.'

Arthur and Terry walked down the hospital corridor, heavily laden with baskets of fruit and rolls of magazines and newspapers.

'You can say what you like,' Arthur muttered. 'It's a good earner.'

'Yes Arthur – I know it. I've worked the shop floor.'

'The voice of experience.'

'Certainly the voice.'

'There are none more gullible than your average punter,' said Arthur philosophically.

'Don't start,' warned Terry. 'The old boy needs a rest.'

'I'm very sensitive to that,' admonished Arthur. 'I've been ill myself. Remember?'

'I remember,' said Terry.

'Anyway, it was a nice little number.'

'Yeah.'

'You like the gee-gees?'

'That's why I'm skint.'

'You've always got on with dumb animals –'

They were now walking down the ward – towards an empty bed.

'My Gawd!'

'He's gone,' said Terry reverently as they stared down at where T.P. had been. 'I wonder if St Peter *does* take credit cards.'

'Eh?'

'Nothing, Arthur.'

'He was a great man, an inspirer of souls.'

'He certainly inspired you.'

'A backroom boy – of course.'

156

'Of course.'

'But I'm grateful to him.'

'Yeah.'

'What about a wreath, Terry?'

'What about one?'

'You'll have to sub me.'

'*What*?'

'Well – he didn't deliver before he went.'

'P'raps it was sudden, Arthur.'

'He could have set us up for another week.' Arthur sounded very aggrieved. 'He could at least have done that.'

'Arthur, you're a –'

'Hallo, you two scallywags.'

'No,' said Arthur. 'It's a voice from the grave – from beyond.'

They both turned to see T.P. in a wheelchair, pushed by his daughter, Fenella.

'Where's me money, Arthur?' asked T.P. with a wry smile.

Recovering from the immediate shock, Arthur said:

'You look so well.'

'Got to move on.'

'Where to?'

'Switzerland.'

'What happens there?' asked Terry, looking at Fenella, She shrugged and her Father replied, 'Expensive clinics and an awful lot of banks.'

'It's not my idea,' Fenella said.

'You'll get nicked,' Terry replied.

'I'll tell you what,' said Mooney to Arthur.

'Yes my old mate?' Arthur's voice was warm with bonhomie.

'I'll phone you.'

PART FOUR

'God rest his soul.'

Arthur adjusted his black tie, whilst Terry opened the door of the Jag for him.

'You all right, Arthur?'

'I'm in mourning, Terence.'

'What? For Jimmy South?'

'It was a tragic end.'

'To be found upside down in a cement works? Nasty!'

'Don't talk about it now, Terry,' Arthur said in a hushed and reverent voice. 'It's not decent.'

'You hated him.'

'I respected him.'

'He was the biggest villain on the manor.'

'He was misguided,' said Arthur sadly. 'He had strayed from the rocky path we all have to tread.'

'Some go piggy-back,' muttered Terry as they watched the last of the mourners leaving the Wembley Crematorium. A thin drizzle was descending on their subdued clothing, except in a few cases, where umbrellas protected white, smug faces. Arthur sat in the back of the Jaguar and lit a cigar. He shuddered.

'Death worries me, Tel.'

' Not ready to meet your Maker yet, Arthur?'

'I've too much to do to go yet.'

'We none of us know when we'll be called,' intoned Terry.

Arthur shuddered again.

'With my health –' he began.

' 'Allo.'

'What's up?'

'Here comes the second biggest villain on the manor.'

'Oh my Gawd!' Arthur looked uneasy as a large man appeared with a shining bald pate. He wore a black astrakhan coat and carried a parasol – an eccentricity that made him somehow deeply sinister. 'Tommy La Roche!'

'Wonder what he wants with you, Arthur?'

'He can't want anything,' snapped Arthur. 'I didn't have no business with him – so what can I do for his partner?'

'P'raps he's just coming over to thank you for your condolences, Arthur.'

'Yeah, that's it. We sent a nice wreath.'

'It would've been, if it hadn't been a florist's reject.'

'I'm not a rich man,' said Arthur, 'not like Jim. Besides, it's the thought that counts.'

La Roche knocked on the window of the Jag, as a light rain mist began to descend on the crematorium gardens. Arthur wound down the window, smiling artificially.

'Hallo, Arthur.' La Roche's voice was gravelly, expressionless.

'Mr La Roche. Good to see you – but I regret the occasion.'

La Roche said nothing and there was an uneasy silence, broken only by the muffled sound of traffic.

'You did a bit of business with Jimmy recently,' said La Roche eventually.

'Me?'

'Come on, Arthur, spit it out.'

'I didn't do no business with him. But I might have done him a favour.'

'What favour?'

'I rented some storage space to him.'

'Oh yeah?'

'Weeks back.'

La Roche cleared his throat and a smell of damp grass wafted into the car.

'I had it spare,' said Arthur.

'What did he put there?'

'Now, I couldn't answer that,' replied Arthur. 'I always respect confidentiality.'

'Eh?' La Roche came nearer, sticking his head through the window. We got trouble, thought Terry. Maybe not now, but definitely later, unless Arthur plays ball. But he didn't.

'I don't know what he put there.'

'It's your space, Arthur,' said La Roche.

'Look,' said Arthur, 'Jim came to me for a favour – like they all do.'

'I'm sure they do,' said La Roche, his voice a little harder.

'I don't enquire.'

'I see. But it's there now, is it?'

'No.'

162

'What?'

Arthur bowed his head reverently. 'It was the last time I saw Jim. When he came and removed the goods.'

'When was this?'

'Couple of days before his tragic end.' Arthur's voice trembled a little.

'You there when he took 'em?' asked La Roche.

'No, sir.'

'You just let people go in and out of your lock-up without a by-your-leave?'

'In some cases.'

'How do they get in?'

'I let them have a key.'

'Did he return it?'

'He did, God bless him.'

La Roche smiled quickly. Then he said, 'I'll be in touch, Arthur.'

'Always ready to see a pal of Jimmy's,' replied Arthur with a sickly smile.

Slowly, La Roche walked away and soon he was lost in the damp, cotton-wool atmosphere. Once he had gone, Arthur drew up his coat collar and said to Terry, 'Get me out of here.'

'What's up, Arthur? Someone walk over your grave?' asked Terry thoughtfully.

'Don't joke about death,' said Arthur. 'It's no laughing matter.'

'Who's joking?' returned Terry.

'What's up, Arthur?' Terry repeated as he pulled the Jag up in front of Arthur's flat. Arthur had been strangely quiet in the back of the car and his cigar had gone out. He looked damp and subdued.

'Nothing, Tel. Death affects me – I'm a sensitive man.'

'There's more to it than that, Arthur.'

'Eh?'

'Why don't you come clean?'

'I told you, Terry – I have respect for the grim reaper.'

'La Roche has rattled you, hasn't he?'

'Now why should he do that?'

'What have you really done with Jimmy's stuff? I

remember it coming in – but I don't remember it going out.'

'You can't be privy to all my affairs, Terence. I'm a busy man.'

'You're a frightened one.'

'Terence.' Arthur stared at him from the plush interior of the back of the car. He looked crushed and out of sorts. 'You must not try to interpret my feelings.'

'I know you, Arthur.'

'Who do you think you are? An agony aunt?'

Terry shrugged. 'You don't want me to hang around?'

'No thank you.'

'Sure?'

'Yes. I want to be alone.'

'Touch of the Garbo's eh?'

'You don't understand, Terry. A man has died in the prime of life. I wish to cogitate.'

'That sounds nasty.'

Arthur frowned. 'Death has no dominion, Terry.'

'Eh?'

'I'm afraid that's above your head, old son.'

'Arthur –'

'Yeah?'

'Wasn't Jimmy about your age?'

'I beg your pardon!'

'Wasn't Jimmy about your age when he croaked?'

'I didn't realise my age was such public knowledge.'

'I could make a pretty good guess at it – and I knew Jim's.'

Arthur hauled himself out of the back of the Jag and stood on the pavement, a crumpled figure in a hired black suit. 'Good night to you, Terry. I shall now spend some time in quiet thought and meditation.'

He walked slowly into the house while Terry stared after him quizzically. What was up? he wondered. He had never seen Arthur so subdued – or was he just plain scared?

'Where's Arthur?' Dave asked Terry two days later in the Winchester Club.

'That's the question I was gonna ask you.'

'I haven't seen him – which is very, very strange for a man of unabstemious habits.'

'I've spoken to him on the blower.'

'Is he ill?'

'No – he said he was staying at home for a bit.'

'With 'er indoors? What's he done – fallen in love all over again? Are they having a second honeymoon?'

'I don't think that's a safe bet, Dave.'

'Then, what?'

'I think he's had a bit of a run in with La Roche.'

Dave whistled. 'That could be nasty. I didn't think Arthur was mixed up with the likes of him.'

'We went to Jimmy South's funeral.'

'So did all the crooks in London.'

'Thanks.'

'And half the filth.'

'Yeah, well it's not the filth he's afraid of.'

'Afraid?'

'He's running scared, Dave. Seems Jimmy dumped some stuff on him a couple of days before he croaked.'

'You know what it was?'

'No – but I saw a stack of crates in the lock-up.'

'Then?'

'Then they were gone.'

'And La Roche wants 'em?'

'Something like that.'

'You reckon Jimmy took 'em out?'

'I don't know. I've got an awful feeling he didn't.'

'Because he croaked?'

'Yeah.'

'And so Arthur – disposed of 'em? Would he have been fool enough to do that?'

'You know Arthur.'

'And now?'

'He's lying low.'

'So what now?'

'I dunno. But I'm gonna keep an eye on the lock-up.'

'What about La Roche?'

'He might come around for a little look-see.'

Dave poured out two large scotches and gave one to Terry.

'What's this? A celebration?'

'Thought you might need a bit of Dutch courage,' said Dave.

'Blimey.'

The lock-up was a scene of complete devastation. Nearly every crate and package had been overturned and ripped open and the contents strewn around the floor. The filing cabinet had been up-ended and, once again, most of its contents had been either scattered around or torn up – as if someone had finally lost their temper at the end of a fruitless search. Terry stared at the wreckage, making up his mind that he would have to go and invade Arthur's meditation in the flat. But as he was walking out, some sixth sense made him step back inside. He was too late, however, to close the door and the two heavies came in fast.

'What the hell do you want?' asked Terry, looking at the knife one of them carried in his outstretched hand.

'Just a bit of information.'

'What about?'

'Your boss.'

'So –'

'He had a pile of crates in here a few days ago.'

'Did he?'

The man with the knife advanced slightly. He was in his late thirties, heavily built with a rather fussy little beard. His colleague was younger.

'Yeah – he did. Now they're gone.'

'I'll take your word for that.'

'We want to know where they are.'

'They belong to a friend.'

'They would. Well?' He advanced again, holding the knife out threateningly.

Terry looked round him. 'I thought you'd already had a look-see for yourselves.'

'We did.'

'Then you know there ain't no crates.'

'We thought we'd ask you.'

'I can tell you nothing.'

'No?' The man came a few steps nearer Terry.

'You sure?'

'Yeah.'

Terry poised, ready for trouble he knew was coming. Then he heard the sound of distant police sirens. Both of the heavies paused – and the sirens came nearer.

'We'll be in touch,' said the man with the beard and they disappeared abruptly through the door.

I bet you will, thought Terry as he heard the sound of a hastily revving engine. A few seconds later, the sound of the sirens intensified and there was a squeal of tyres outside the lock-up.

'Here we are again,' said Terry philosophically.

'Arthur had a bit of a clean-out?' asked Detective Inspector Chisholm.

'I dunno – I just got 'ere!'

'Oh yes?'

'It's all a bit surprise to me.'

'It would be,' Chisholm looked around him gloomily picking up a cluster of black knickers. 'Fell off the back of a camel?' he asked.

'I wouldn't know,' said Terry firmly.

'Anything missing?'

'Arthur knows the stock.'

'And where is Mr Daley?'

'At home – he's not too well.'

'I am sorry about that. Arthur's got quite a delicate constitution nowadays, hasn't he? What with one thing and another.'

Looking around him cautiously, Arthur left his flat and walked the few yards to his Jag. Once inside it he felt safe, but on the streets he knew he was only too exposed. With a sigh of relief, he inserted the key in the door, climbed in and sat behind the wheel, his eyes closed and his breathing deep.

'Hallo, Arthur.'

'Oh my Gawd!' For a moment Arthur felt as if he was

having the major coronary he had always feared. He couldn't breathe and his whole body was bathed in an instant cold sweat.

'Nice to see you out and about again.'

Arthur made an inarticulate noise that sounded like the bleating of a wounded animal.

'Now we want you to drive us.'

'Where?' Arthur managed in a falsetto.

'To see a man about some crates.'

'I don't know nothing about any crates.'

'No, well p'raps the drive will help your memory.'

Arthur switched on the ignition, ground the gears and the Jag leapt forward uncertainly.

'Don't try anything, Arthur,' said the man in the back patiently.

'I'm not.'

'Just nervous are we?'

'I'm not a well man. I mustn't be subjected to any strain – doctor's orders.'

'Oh dear. Well, I'm sure we'll all make this as little of a strain as possible.'

'Where am I going?'

'Down Wapping way, Arthur, just to have a good look at old Father Thames.'

Ten minutes later, Arthur brought the Jag to a shaky halt outside a boarded up pub. A crude sign stated 'DUKE'S DEMOLITION LTD' and he could hear the rattling of a compressor.

'This is where we get out,' said the man in the back. 'You'll not try a runner, will you, Arthur?'

'Who – me?'

"Cos if you do, I've got a little automatic here, with a silencer – and I'll kneecap you – and that won't be a nice experience, will it?

Slowly, Arthur clambered out of the Jag, shadowed by his stowaway. Once on the pavement, Arthur turned to see a slim young man with a punk hair-do and a broken nose.

'Where we going?' asked Arthur.

'The old Red Lion. Sorry the bar's closed, but I'd be obliged if you'd enter by the saloon door.'

Arthur cautiously entered the building to find daylight streaming in from where the roof had been and most of the partitions already demolished.

'Down there.'

The young man pointed down a flight of rickety stairs that were covered in debris.

'That's not safe,' said Arthur.

'Neither am I, Dad. Now move it.'

Arthur stumbled down the stairs into the darkness below.

'She says he went off in the Jag,' said Chisholm, emerging from Arthur's flat. 'Been hanging round her feet for a couple of days.'

'He's not been well,' said Terry defensively.

'No?'

'Been under a lot of strain recently.'

'Course he has. But I happen to know Arthur's been looking after something for somebody. At least he was for a bit.'

'I'm not with you.'

'A certain somebody who's unfortunately recently deceased.'

'You mean Jimmy South?'

'Clever boy.'

'What would Arthur have of Jimmy South's? He was too big for him.'

'Oh this is only small. But small enough to be interesting.'

'Well,' said Terry, 'Arthur will surface somewhere.'

'He might not do that, my old son.'

'Why not?'

'Arthur's done a naughty to the South mob. They won't like that.'

'Jimmy's dead.'

'Don't be naive, Terry.'

'You mean his mates?'

'So let's drop in at the Winchester. We might find Arthur's taken refuge there.'

'Refuge?'

'Terry – there's something you should know.' Detective Inspector Chisholm smiled sweetly.

'What's that?'

'Arthur's on the run – well and truly on the one foot in front of the other caper.'

'What are you gonna do about it?'

'I want to see where he runs.'

The cellar was almost in complete darkness when Arthur managed, with some assistance, to descend the steps. Once there, he groped his way to a wall and hung on to it, breathing heavily. The place smelt of stale beer and other substances, vaguely animal in origin. For a while, there was almost total silence until the young man said, 'Switch on the light, Arthur.'

'Eh?'

'It's just to your right.'

Obediently, Arthur groped against the wall, feeling the light brush of cobwebs and the patter of a spider as it ran over his hand. He almost screamed aloud.

'What's up?'

'Bloody spiders!'

There was a throaty chuckle from somewhere else in the cellar and Arthur realised that there was another person in there with them. It was not a pleasant thought.

'He's not been here for three days,' said Dave.

'Funny – 'er indoors said he left in the Jag,' replied Terry while Chisholm merely looked frustrated.

'Maybe he had some business to attend to,' said Chisholm. 'He'd have wanted to tank up.'

'How you misjudge the man,' sighed Dave.

Chisholm grunted. 'I've never misjudged Arthur,' he replied.

'There's always a first time,' mumbled Dave.

Arthur eventually found the light switch and the cellar was flooded with a dim, yellowish light. At first there was no sign of anyone else – just heaped-up beer crates, an old pump, a

170

battered horsehair sofa with the horsehair leaking out, and a couple of old and rusting Aladdin stoves. Once again Arthur heard the throaty chuckle.

'Well, Arthur,' said the young man, 'feeling ready to meet an old friend?'

'What's going on?' shrilled Arthur. 'I'm a respectable business man. I can't be lured down to cellars.'

'Why not, Arthur?' asked a familiar voice. 'You're neither respectable nor are you a business man.'

'I'll have you know –' Arthur began indignantly. Then he exclaimed: 'Oh my Gawd!' The colour drained from his cheeks and a muscle in his right cheek began to twitch. 'Oh my Gawd!' he cried again and began to shake.

'There's no need to call on the Deity, Arthur. I'm sure I can answer most of the more immediate questions about your future.'

Jimmy South stepped out from behind a screen, smiling gently at Arthur.

Chisholm and Terry were standing outside the Winchester.

'He's in dead trouble, Terry.'

'With you?'

'No – with the South mob. They'll take him apart.'

'What's he done?'

'The whisper is that Arthur flogged the South crates when he heard Jimmy had snuffed it.'

'Arthur wouldn't do a thing like that.'

'Wouldn't he?'

Terry was silent.

'Look,' said Chisholm, 'find him. Quick.'

'You're dead,' whimpered Arthur.

'Officially.'

'What do you mean?'

'What I say, Arthur. I'm officially dead.'

'I saw you burn. I was at your funeral.'

'You saw a coffin slide out. I wasn't in it.'

'Who was?'

'No-one who need concern you, Arthur.'

'I can't believe it.'

'I'm alive, Arthur – and I want those video recorders.'

'Eh?'

'Come on – where are they?'

'I don't know nothing about 'em.' Arthur made a pathetic attempt at recovery. 'I must say, it's good to see you looking so well, Jim.'

'Shut up, Arthur.'

'You were too young to die.'

'Where are they?'

'I don't know –'

Jimmy South advanced a few paces towards Arthur.

'You remember me delivering them to you, don't you?'

'Yeah.'

'They're not there now.'

'They must have been nicked.'

'By you.'

'Look, Jim, I was looking after them recorders – if they're gone –'

'Which they have.'

'Someone must have broken into my lock-up and nicked 'em. Person, or persons unknown.'

'Not unknown, Arthur.'

'Eh?'

'We know the person – it's you.'

'But –'

'You sold 'em to Danny Foster, didn't you?'

'Look Jim –'

'Didn't you?'

'I certainty didn't,' said Arthur feebly.

'Because Danny Foster says you did.'

'He's lying.'

'No way.'

'I deny –'

'And he gave you five grand, didn't he?'

'I wish to state here and now –'

'So where's the five grand, Arthur?'

Suddenly Arthur collapsed and sat down heavily on a beer crate.

'I spent it,' he said.

'You what?'

'I had some debts –'

'Five grand's worth?'

'Thereabouts.'

'Who to?'

'Micky the Monk. I owed him – took a lot of stuff on sale or return. And he wouldn't take it back.'

'I'm not interested, Arthur. You heard I'd bought it – and flogged the stuff. Now I want the money.'

'I'll get it back for you,' said Arthur desperately.

'From Micky? You won't have a chance.'

'I'll get it some other way.'

'You will an' all – because I've had a few little problems.'

'Like being dead?' said Arthur recklessly.

'I don't like jokers,' said Jimmy, 'they're liable to get cut up.'

Arthur said nothing.

'I needed to be dead, right? Too many of 'em closing in. So – I was off to the Canary Islands with a new I.D.'

'Very pleasant climate.'

'I'm sure it is, Arthur, but I may not get there.'

'Why not, Jim?' said Arthur. 'You're a resourceful man.'

'I know I am, Arthur. But someone let me down over money. Now I need that five grand for travelling expenses. Get it?'

'Yeah.'

'I'll give you forty-eight hours, Arthur.'

'What?'

'Find the dough, Arthur. I can hold out here for forty-eight hours. No longer.'

'But I know where the stuff's gone – you've got to believe me, Jim.'

Jim South looked across at the young man with the beard.

'This conversation's getting repetitive.'

The young man with the beard walked slowly across to Arthur and then with great precision took him by the throat.

'The position is this, Arthur. Jim needs the money in forty-eight hours.'

173

Arthur made a rattling sound as the young man increased the pressure on his windpipe.

'And *you* have to *find* the money in forty-eight hours.' He increased the pressure. 'If you don't – I'll kill you.'

He suddenly released him and Arthur fell to the floor, gasping for breath.

Jimmy South grinned down at him. 'Happy hunting, Arthur.'

A few hours later, Arthur strode into the Winchester with all the bonhomie of a desperate man.

'Where the hell have you been?' yelled Terry. 'We thought you'd been kidnapped.'

Arthur smiled icily. 'Now what gave you that idea?'

'You went to earth, Arthur,' said Dave.

'Oh yeah?'

'Even Chisholm's been making fond enquiries.'

'I find that very touching.'

'So where have you been, Arthur?' asked Terry. 'I've searched everywhere for you.'

'I find that very touching too, Tel.'

'Shut up, Arthur.'

Arthur put an avuncular arm around Terry's shoulders.

'My dear boy – I've been in conference.'

'You've been hiding out with 'er indoors.'

'That was thinking time.'

'I see. What's up?'

'Something rather special.'

'Oh yeah?'

'A good work!'

'From you?'

Arthur laid a printed handbill on the bar in front of Terry and Dave. I read:

SAVE THE KILIKO INDIANS
DON'T LET THEM DIE
£5,000 WILL SAVE THIS
PRIMITIVE TRIBE OF THE SOUTH
AMERICAN RAIN FORESTS.

GRAND SPONSORED BATH-TUB
JOURNEY. SPONSOR TERRY McCANN
AS HE ROWS A BATH-TUB UP AND
DOWN THE LENGTH OF OLD FATHER
THAMES.

SAVE THE KILIKO INDIANS
DON'T LET THEM DIE

Terry looked up from the handbill, his eyes almost popping out of his head.

'No,' he said. 'No!'

'Come on, Tel,' said Arthur admonishingly. 'A big, strong lad like you, and you won't take part in one of the most important conservation projects of our time.'

'That's right, I won't.'

'Shame on you.'

'What's in it for you, Arthur?'

'I beg your pardon?'

'I *said* – what's in it for you?'

'I don't understand. I would have thought it was obvious.'

'You collect five grand – and send it to South America?'

'I told you, it's a good work.'

'You've never done a good work in your life, Arthur,' said Dave blandly.

Arthur looked shocked. 'How can you say a terrible thing like that?' he asked.

'Because it's true,' said Terry.

'I'm very hurt, Terence. As a prominent local businessman I've done my fair bit for charity.'

'When?'

'And now I have my chance to contribute to world aid.'

'Who are these Kiliko Indians?' asked Dave.

'They were drawn to my attention by a prominent anthropologist.'

'Who?' said Terry.

'He advised me of their need.'

'What is their need, Arthur?' asked Dave.

'They're on the way out – dying from a common virus. They need medicine – fast.'

175

'Five grand won't do much,' said Terry.

'It's but a small contribution,' said Arthur. 'Prominent businessmen up and down the country have been asked to raise the money – amounting to millions. I feel a duty incumbent on myself as a man of charity – of benevolence.'

'Then why don't *you* get in the bath-tub?'

'Don't be foolish, Terence. I'm not a fit man – like yourself.'

'I'm not doing it, Arthur.'

'It is your duty. Children are dying, they need the antidote.'

Terry paused. 'Who approached you?'

'Professor Eisemeyer.'

'Who the hell is he?'

'I told you – a distinguished anthropologist.'

'And he's approached other people?'

'He has – prominent businessmen, like myself. Men renowned for their liberal outlook, their compassion and their inventiveness.'

'You've got that all right, Arthur,' said Terry.

'So the least you can do is to get in the bath-tub.'

Terry was silent. Then he said, 'How you gonna raise the dibs?'

'Multi-national companies. Conservation groups.' Arthur airily waved his handbill.

'So where do I go?'

'You'll do it?'

Terry grinned. 'I hope it's for a good cause, Arthur.'

'What better than preventing the suffering of little ones?'

'You're very noble, Arthur,' said Dave. He blew his nose noisily.

Terry said: 'How many weeks have we got?'

'Eh?'

'How many weeks we got to book the sponsors – and for me to train?'

Arthur laughed. 'You don't seem to realise the urgency of the children's needs.'

'So?'

Arthur looked at his watch. 'It's three fifteen.'

'Yeah?'

'You start at five.'

'What?'

'Terry – will you stop being selfish?'

'Arthur – this is bloody ridiculous!'

'Even now a small child is gasping for breath in a jungle.'

'Where?'

'Every minute counts.'

'But the money –'

'Will be pledged in the next few hours.'

'Who by?'

'My own business contacts.'

'They couldn't raise daisies.'

'Leave that to me, Terry. The ceremonial start will be from Wapping Step at five. Be there, Terence, and dress suitably.'

Arthur downed the last of his vodka and strode from the bar, leaving a bewildered Terry to say to Dave:

'Do you think he's finally gone off his block?'

'This is London Sounds on One Nine Six.'

Arthur sat behind the microphone, while the producer introduced him to the disc jockey.

'This is Sammy Styles, Mr Daley. He'll be interviewing you.'

'Pleased to meet you.'

'Hallo, Arthur. Good of you to come on the programme.'

'It's a pleasure.'

'Fascinating cause, isn't it?'

'It certainly is – and an urgent one.'

'Yes – I gather they're dropping like flies. Now pledges will be coming in during the course of the show and I gather we're going over live to Wapping Steps to see your noble paddler off on his journey. Tell me, Arthur, are you really expecting him to circumnavigate the Thames in a day and a night?'

'A night and a day actually, Sammy. Well – you know we hope he'll be sponsored for every mile he completes, so we'll just have to see how well he does. I don't expect miracles – but he will be paddling through the night.'

'O.K., Arthur. Now the light's coming up and I'm going to chat to you on the air. Righteho?'

'Righteho,' said Arthur, lighting his cigar.

'This is London Sounds One Nine Six – welcome to the Sammy Styles Show.' He played a burst of music. 'And my first guest is prominent London business man, Arthur Daley, who is organising a bit of Marathon Thames paddling in aid of relief for the Kiliko Indians of South America. Arthur – tell us all about it.'

Arthur cleared his throat. 'Thank you Sammy. It's good to be on the prog. Well – it's all a bit of a dash because the needs of the Kiliko are immediate. My colleague, Terry McCann is going to have a bit of fun paddling up the Thames in a bath-tub.' He laughed heartily, joined by Sammy. 'It's quite a sight,' Arthur commented.

'Is he gonna give himself a scrub as he goes?' asked Sammy jocularly.

'There won't be time for that kind of thing,' replied Arthur, as both Sammy and the producer winced.

'We want sponsorship by the hour – right up until the deadline of tomorrow midnight.'

'And that's a must,' said Sammy, 'or these Indians will not receive sufficient medical aid. And what will happen to them, Arthur?'

With a catch in his voice, Arthur said quietly: 'It's quite simple, Sammy – they'll die.'

'I see – well, we can't let that happen that's for sure. Can I ask you, Arthur, is this only the tip of the iceberg?'

'Yes – I just happen to have got it together quicker than anyone else, for over the next few months, professional business men like myself will be sponsoring other events in aid of these simple people, who stand in such deadly danger from a Western imported virus.'

'It's good to know that there are people around like you, Arthur, who are prepared to put their energy into such an important piece of conservation.'

'I'm for people,' said Arthur, 'I'm just into them.'

'Yes,' said Sammy Styles, 'it's pure humanity at work. And I hope you are all going to support the bath-tub rescue. Because I certainly am. O.K., Arthur, where do they get their sponsorship forms from?'

'From the foyer of your own radio station – and from the departure point at Wapping Steps.'

'And we hope you come in your thousands. Arthur Daley – human being par excellence – the very best of luck to you.'

'Thank you,' said Arthur. 'Thank you, one and all.'

The D.J. played a record and turned to Arthur.

'Bully for you, mate.'

Arthur drew a xeroxed sponsorship form out of his pocket and smiled at Sammy.

'Will you be so good?'

'Certainly.'

He scrawled a figure on the form with a flourish. It was not until Arthur was in the producer's office that he saw Sammy had put himself down for 10p a mile. How mean can you get? thought Arthur as the producer said:

'Right, let's see how the foyer situation goes – and then we'll run you down to Wapping in the radio car.'

'Most kind. But I must slip out for half an hour. Got to get something.'

'Anything we can do?'

'I have got to buy a bath,' said Arthur. ' You could bring it down on the roof of your car.'

The producer smiled a little frostily. 'What a good idea,' he said.

'In training, Tel?' asked Dave.

Terry had spent the afternoon in the Winchester and was now on his third lager. 'I'll keep going on booze,' he confided.

'It's good of you to do it.'

'I must be crazy,' he said.

'You know,' said Dave, 'I never thought Arthur would be capable of doing a thing like this.'

'I don't think he is.' replied Terry.

'The bath's in your foyer,' said Arthur to the producer who sighed miserably. 'That's all right, innit?'

'Fine.'

'Then we can strap it to the roof of your radio car and get it down to Wapping.'

'Absolutely fine. One small thing –'

'Yeah?'

'We've had quite a few people coming in for sponsorship forms while you were out.'

'That can't be bad.'

'No, but I notice on the bottom of the form it says that all money must be handed in by midnight tomorrow. That's tricky – he'll just have finished.'

'It's the urgency of the situation. You must appreciate that.'

'Of course.'

'Children may die.'

'Yes.'

'They *will* die unless medical aid can be rushed into the rain forest.'

'I was only querying the sheer practicality of it all.'

'That's all right. I put a notice in your foyer.'

'Did you?'

'Yeah – and I'd be pleased if you'd broadcast it. There's something important I forgot.'

'What's that, Mr Daley?' said the producer with growing tension in his voice.

'I'll be here in person in your foyer from midnight through till dawn – and beyond if necessary. Picking up the sponsorship money. It will be my own personal vigil.'

'I see. Well that's most noble.' He looked at his watch and said, 'I think we'd better get you and your bath-tub down to Wapping.'

'Most kind,' said Arthur.

'I'm sending a reporter with you, of course.'

'It'll be quite an event.'

'Yes,' said the producer, 'it's become that already.'

At five p.m. a small crowd had gathered on Wapping Steps and the bath-tub, with a plastic paddle in it, was bobbing gently by the wharf. Terry stood beside it, wearing a track suit and a life-jacket. He felt particularly foolish. Arthur scurried about the radio car. With him was an attractive young girl with a tape recorder.

'I haven't had time to introduce you to Terry yet,' said Arthur. 'He's just raring to go. Terry may I introduce you to Miss Tracey Jones. She's going to interview you.'

'I'd like to interview you, Arthur,' said Terry.

The bath-tub looked totally unstable and the paddle a child's toy – which it was.

'Now, now,' said Arthur. He turned to Tracey. 'He's full of fun.'

Tracey pushed the microphone into Terry's face and said brightly: 'Terry McCann – you've volunteered for a tough task. What made you do it?'

'I was thinking of all those little children in the South American rain forest – waiting for medical aid.'

'And now you're going to paddle as hard as you can up the Thames in a bath-tub? Are you looking forward to it?'

'It's all great fun.'

'Yes, I'm sure it is – and every mile that Terry paddles more money will be raised for the Kiliko Indians. Well, we've got quite a crowd down here on Wapping Steps and many of them have already received their sponsor forms. Beside me, local business man, Arthur Daley, is dishing out more forms in addition to his many other duties. Arthur Daley, can I just snatch a few words?'

'With the greatest of pleasure.'

'Now, your contribution to this scheme is five thousand pounds – do you hope that Terry will raise all of this?'

'He'd better –' Arthur hastily corrected himself. 'He's going to have a jolly good try. Terry knows that every mile he paddles brings in more money – for the Kiliko Indians and their desperate plight in the Amazon rain forest.'

'Thank you, Arthur Daley. And now Terry McCann is getting into his bath-tub. It's looking bit shaky and so is he – whoops – he nearly had it over, but Mr Daley and some of the spectators are holding it for him – and yes – yes – he's in control. Yes – he's slowly, very slowly – beginning to paddle downstream. He's called out something to Mr Daley – couldn't hear what it was – but there we have to leave the Kiliko Indians sponsored bath-tub marathon and return you to the studio.'

'Arthur,' shouted Terry across the water.

'Well done,' said Arthur, 'keep it up!'

'You didn't put any food on board.'

'No.'

'Or drink.'

'Keep paddling, Tel.'

'I'll starve – or die of thirst.'

'I'll follow you up in the Jag.'

'Where's our meeting place?'

'I'll track you down. I'll bring a couple of pork pies and a bottle of lager.'

'Thank you, Arthur. I'll always remember your generosity.'

He began to turn in circles again and Arthur shouted at him urgently, 'Get on course.'

'It's not easy, Arthur.'

'Straighten up.'

Terry said something quietly that Arthur did not hear. One of the spectators did, however, and there was a flurry of laughter as she repeated it to her friends. Suddenly a big motor-boat hove into view and began to bear down on Terry in his tub. Arthur watched it for a few moments with mounting excitement.

'BBC, I expect,' he said to Tracey. 'I phoned 'em you know.'

'Don't see any cameras,' she said.

'Or the press. I called 'em all.'

'Aren't they a bit near?'

'Near?'

'Yes, they're causing such a wash, they'll have him over.'

'Oi,' yelled Arthur, 'they're too near.'

'They're still running at him.'

'Change course, you idiots,' shouted Arthur.

The crowd also screamed out, but the big motor cruiser did not alter course at all.

'It's going to hit him,' said Tracey.

A few seconds before the impact, Terry looked up to see a slightly, but not instantly recognisable, face ducking down behind the cock-pit cover of the cruiser. As it rammed him amidships, Terry recognised that slightly familiar face. It was La Roche.

'He's a goner,' said Arthur fatalistically as the cruiser buried both the bath and Terry in a curl of foam.

'He didn't have time to jump,' yelled Tracey as the crowd became hysterical.

'My Terry,' moaned Arthur. 'My poor brave lad.'

The cruiser ploughed on with a considerable turn of speed and began to roar away, leaving a wake behind it that dashed itself against the wharf, soaking the onlookers.

'Get the police,' someone shouted. But Arthur's attention was only on the surface of the water. It bore no sign of either the bath, or Terry.

Desperately fighting for breath, Terry swam under the hull of the cruiser, diving deep again to avoid the deadly thrust of the propellor. For a moment he thought he was finished as he received a glancing blow to the head that almost knocked him unconscious. Then he felt himself rising and he struck out for the surface, feeling at any moment his lungs would burst. After what seemed like an eternity of pain he finally broke through the grey suffocating water and once again saw the London skyline.

He also saw Arthur, standing on the wharf, his head bowed.

Choking and spitting out water, Terry shouted:

'All right, Arthur, no need for another funeral!'

'Well – that was short-lived,' said Tracey as she helped haul the sodden and bleeding Terry onto the wharf-side.

Arthur shrugged. 'I've had it.'

'What do you mean?'

'You can always organise it for another time,' said Tracey.

'Eh?' said Terry, still bringing up water.

'The ambulance will be here soon,' she said in a jolly voice.

'What's that you –' he spluttered, looking up at Arthur.

'It'll be too late,' said Arthur. 'Too late for the rescue.' He looked as if his last hour had come. 'It's my funeral,' he said to Terry.

*

'How are you feeling?' asked Dave as Terry drank a large brandy.

'Fine.'

'They kept you in overnight?'

'Only to put a few stitches in the cranium.'

'No brain damage?'

'Nothing to damage. There can't be after the things I do for Arthur.'

'Chisholm's been here.'

'Oh yeah?'

'He's gone to fetch Arthur.'

'Where is he?'

'Hiding behind her vacuum cleaner, no doubt.'

'I wonder why –'

'What's that?'

'Never mind.' Terry turned to the door. 'Talk of the devil!' Chisholm came in with a beaming Arthur.

'How are you Tel?' Arthur asked, putting his arm round his shoulders.

'Apart from nearly drowning and nearly getting a fractured skull – great! Why are you looking so cheerful?'

'It's always good news,' said Arthur, 'when villains are brought to justice.'

Chisholm smiled. 'Had a bit of a coup,' he said.

'What's that?' asked Dave.

'I'm about to tell you something in confidence,' said Chisholm. 'And I'll come down like a ton of bricks on anyone who takes all this further than this room.'

'I'm the soul of discretion,' said Dave.

'Likewise,' put in Terry.

'Mm – well Arthur knows.'

'And I'm a trustworthy client,' said Arthur smugly. Terry and Dave raised their eyebrows.

'When thieves fall out,' said Chisholm, 'fun begins for us coppers.'

'Give us more,' asked Terry.

'Well – the late lamented Jimmy South ain't dead after all.'

'What?' said Terry, staggered. 'I saw him cremated!'

'Appears he faked the death to get out of the country fast. Matters were pressing.'

'Who was in the coffin?' asked Dave.

'Some minor villain they wanted to top. Anyway, Jim was holed up by one of his associates in the East End while they got some money together to send him out.'

'What then?' asked Dave.

'We got a call last night saying where he was – someone grassed him so we went and picked him up. Simple as that.'

'Who grassed him?'

'Haven't the faintest. But the whisper says Jim fell out with one of his partners. So they didn't want him to leave the Mother Country any more. Thought I'd tell Arthur – as he was having a bit of trouble with 'im.' Chisholm looked round him as Dave said:

'Can I offer you a half, Mr Chisholm?'

'You can, David. I think this calls for a small celebration.'

Terry looked across to Arthur's cheerful countenance.

'You celebrating too, Arthur?'

Arthur smiled sadly. 'I'm a charitable man,' he said, 'no-one's gonna be celebrating in the rain forest, are they?'

'But a villain has been brought to justice, Arthur,' said Chisholm. 'I'm sure you'll drink to that.'

'I'll always drink to that, Mr Chisholm,' replied Arthur blandly.

Minder

– back again

Anthony Masters

Terry McCann and Arthur Daley are the Laurel and Hardy of
London's criminal fraternity. Arthur's the one with the silver
tongue, he could talk his way past St. Peter at the pearly gates
if he wanted to. They say he even charges his mum petrol
money when he runs her home . . . And when Arthur's hot air
finally blows cold, it's usually poor old Terry who's left to do
the dirty work! If there's ever a fast buck to be made, they'll be
there like a shot. The only trouble is, where Terry and Arthur
are concerned, there's always a sting in the tale as well!

MINDER – BACK AGAIN is based on the smash hit Thames
Television series created by Leon Griffiths, starring Dennis
Waterman and George Cole.

TV TIE-IN/FICTION   0 7221 5823 8   £1.50

Also by Anthony Masters, available in Sphere paperback:

MINDER

BACHELOR BOYS

THE YOUNG ONES'

BOOK

BEN ELTON · LISE MAYER · RIK MAYALL

Call it bad karma or anarchy in the U.K., there's never been anything quite like the cult-hit T.V. series *The Young Ones* — totally bizarre, totally original, totally aggressive and . . . totally TOTAL. So, here are the Young Ones in their own write at last: Rick the Radical Poet, Vyvyan the Psychopathic Punk, Neil the Suicidal Hippy, and Mike, the Would-Be Spiv. Together they reveal The Ultimate Truth About Everything to their avid fans, including absolutely zillions of helpless hints on:

★ HOBBIES
Neil's 101 really interesting things to do with a tea-cup
★ FILTH
Some kissing hints from Vyvyan. Lesson one: Snog the Dog
★ LAUGHS
Including Rick's only joke: These are my pants and I'm sticking to them!!!
PLUS
a controversial statement from the Acne Liberation Front. The Young Ones say: WEAR YOUR SPOTS WITH PRIDE

NON-FICTION/HUMOUR   0 7221 5765 7   £2.95

A selection of bestsellers from SPHERE

FICTION

DEEP SIX	Clive Cussler	£2.25 ☐
MILLENNIUM	John Varley	£1.99 ☐
SMART WOMEN	Judy Blume	£2.25 ☐
INHERITORS OF THE STORM	Victor Sondheim	£2.95 ☐
HEADLINES	Bernard Weinraub	£2.75 ☐

FILM & TV TIE-INS

THE RIVER	Steven Bauer	£1.95 ☐
WATER	Gordon McGill	£1.75 ☐
THE DUNE STORYBOOK	Joan D. Vinge	£2.50 ☐
NO-ONE KNOWS WHERE		
GOBO GOES	Mark Saltzman	£1.50 ☐
BOOBER FRAGGLE'S CELERY		
SOUFFLÉ	Louise Gikow	£1.50 ☐

NON-FICTION

PAUL ERDMAN'S MONEY		
GUIDE	Paul Erdman	£2.95 ☐
THE 1985 FAMILY WELCOME GUIDE		
	Jill Foster and Malcolm Hamer	£3.95 ☐
THE OXFORD CHILDREN'S DICTIONARY		
	John Weston and Alan Spooner	£3.25 ☐
THE WOMAN BOOK OF LOVE AND SEX		
	Deidre Sanders	£1.95 ☐
INTO THE REMOTE PLACES	Ian Hibell with	
	Clinton Trowbridge	£2.95 ☐

All Sphere books are available at your local bookshop or newsagent, or can be ordered direct from the publisher. Just tick the titles you want and fill in the form below.

Name_____

Address_____

_____

Write to Sphere Books, Cash Sales Department, P.O. Box 11, Falmouth, Cornwall TR10 9EN

Please enclose cheque or postal order to the value of the cover price plus:

UK: 55p for the first book, 22p for the second book and 14p per copy for each additional book ordered to a maximum charge of £1.75.

OVERSEAS: £1.00 for the first book and 25p per copy for each additional book.

BFPO & EIRE: 55p for the first book, 22p for the second book plus 14p per copy for the next 7 books, thereafter 8p per book.

Sphere Books reserve the right to show new retail prices on covers which may differ from those previously advertised in the text or elsewhere, and to increase postal rates in accordance with the PO.